THE SWEETEST SONG

The Whinburg Township Amish · Book Nine

ADINA SENFT

Moonshell
Books

"Lord, Who at Cana's Wedding Feast," words by Adelaide Thrupp (1853), music by Gottfried W. Fink (1842), in the public domain.

"The Faithful Carpenter" lyrics © 2015, "Walk a Little While" lyrics © 2021, "I Have Always Seen You" lyrics © 2021 by Shelley Adina Senft Bates. *Er hat ein Weib genommen,* translated by Shelley Adina Senft Bates.

Cover design by Carpe Librum Book Design. Images from Shutterstock, used by permission. Series logo by Jenny Zemanek at Seedlings Online.

The Sweetest Song / Adina Senft—1st ed.

❀ Created with Vellum

For my readers, with gratitude

THE SWEETEST SONG

Yet the Lord will command his lovingkindness in the daytime, and in the night his song shall be with me, and my prayer unto the God of my life. —PSALM 42:8 (KJV)

Willow Creek, Whinburg Township, Pennsylvania
Late December

A wedding was a lot like Christmas, Cora Swarey had always thought. Both involved giving, and family, and a lot of good food. But while the focus of Christmas was on the little baby who would change the world, the focus of a wedding was on the couple who had accepted that little baby into their hearts, and whose vows would change their lives.

She sat at the back of the women's side in the big white tent the Isaac Yoders had rented for the occasion, watching Amanda Yoder and Joshua King say the words that would make them husband and wife. Amanda wore the blue dress and crisp white organdy cape and apron that she'd begun making practically the moment she'd stepped off the train in Lancaster in October. Joshua's white shirt, black pants, and vest and coat had been made by his mother Savilla's loving hands.

"Amanda came home from her summer in Colorado a changed woman," the bride's sister-in-law Sarah Byler, the *Dokterfraa*, had told Cora as they were helping Carrie Miller decorate the wedding cake yesterday. "I don't think it was all Joshua, either. It's as though she became the woman God meant her to be."

"They say that love transforms us," Cora offered, half wondering if she believed it. For her, love had been a consuming fire, leaving her a heap of ashes that she somehow had to turn into a young woman again.

"It does," Sarah allowed, her face glowing as she caught sight of Englisch Henry Byler, her husband, as he set out the twelve coffee mugs he had made as a wedding gift. The handle of each mug formed a different flower, one for each month of the year.

Cora would have given a lot to have even one of those mugs. Their beauty gave her a pain in her heart—a good pain, the kind that came when she heard a red-winged blackbird sing or saw the sun set in glory over the Sangre de Cristo mountain range back home in Colorado. The kind that came when she sang.

But that thought caused pain of an entirely different kind, because she didn't sing anymore. Not her own songs. Her music had gone silent, and she despaired of ever hearing it again.

When her gaze slid toward the men's side where Simon Yoder sat with his young *Aendi*'s male relatives, she controlled the impulse and fixed her attention once more on Amanda and Joshua facing each other at the front of the tent.

"Do you solemnly promise with one another," the bishop

said, looking between them, "that you will love and bear and be patient with each other and shall not separate from each other until dear God shall part you from each other through death?"

"*Ja*, I promise," Amanda said softly, echoing the same vow Joshua had made to her.

Cora's throat ached at the sweet emotion in her friend's face. It was hard to believe they'd only met for the first time in June—a mere six months ago. Joshua's family had moved to the Wet Mountain Valley from Kansas when Cora was a teenager. Some had thought he might choose her, but Cora had known from the beginning that she would always be his sister in Christ, and no more. Besides, back then he had carried a torch for some girl who didn't deserve him in Kansas. Only when Amanda had started work at the Lost Creek Ranch had he realized the torch had burned out and it was time to toss it away. They'd become engaged in October, and then Amanda had come home to Whinburg Township to prepare for their wedding.

Joshua had made a special trip out to the Swarey place just to deliver Amanda's pretty handmade wedding invitation to Cora and her sisters.

"She wants the friends we'll spend our married life with to be there when it begins," Joshua had explained.

So here they were, among the three hundred or so people in the "wedding *haus*," getting down on their knees for the final prayer, and then rising to sing the last hymn.

To sing.

Cora had known since she was a small child that the purpose of raising one's voice in song was to praise *der Herr* who gave it. Not to draw attention to oneself, and certainly not to stand out in any way, but to blend in with the *Gmee* so that all could praise Him with one voice.

By the time Cora was twelve, she had developed two voices. One for church, which for the most part blended in with others, except for those moments when she forgot herself and it soared out above even that of the *Vorsinger*. When that happened, she would damp it down and duck her head so that her red face was hidden behind the girls in front of and beside her. The second voice was for home—in the kitchen, in the barn, out in the vegetable garden, in the *Hinkelhaus* with the chickens.

Many parents, she supposed, would have disciplined her and told her to hold her peace. But Mamm and Dat had never done that, instead enjoying her made-up songs and tunes and sometimes even joining in with the ones that had become familiar to them. Grossmammi on Dat's side had been a singer, too, so it was possible that Cora's caroling around the ranch reminded him of her now that she was gone. Or maybe it was just that for Dat, a woman's voice raised in song was normal.

"It takes the effort of every blade of grass to keep the meadow green," he would say on the way home from church in the buggy, those rare days when she'd embarrassed herself. "But meadows grow the occasional daisy or wild rose. I may not carry fertilizer and a bucket of water out there to make them bigger than they are, but God made them, so why not enjoy them?"

"No fertilizer for me, *denki*," she would reply with a laugh, and feel better, and sing as she helped her younger sisters and Mamm make supper.

Oh yes, she would sing. And then Simon Yoder had come to the ranch this past summer with his friend Joe Byler, and her world had turned inside out.

Well, she would not let him do that to her again. The past was firmly in the past, and forgiven if not forgotten, and he was nothing to her now.

The kitchen helpers departed during the last hymn to make their final preparations for the food to come out. After the bishop blessed the bridal couple, the service was over and Joshua and Amanda King were surrounded by their families and carried away outside so that the men could transform the house of worship into the dining room.

Cora pulled her wool coat more closely around her as she and the other single women filed out behind the married women, and then from inside the tent came the familiar racket of benches being turned around and tables being set up. When the noise died down, she was handed a pile of neatly folded white tablecloths and she and Hannah Riehl and several other girls paired up and got busy laying them over the tables. Unfold—snap open—down. Over and over again, on dozens of long tables. Once that was done, the tables were set with the china and cutlery from the wedding bench wagon. At a walking pace, the young women moved down the aisles, laying down plates one after the other. Since this was her first time helping at an Amish wedding, Hannah followed Cora and her stack of plates with a basket full of cutlery wrapped in sage green paper napkins tied with royal blue ribbon—Amanda's wedding colors—laying a bundle next to each plate. Then came cups and saucers, and jars full of celery, and last of all, every six places, the centerpieces. Amanda's parents, apparently, had consulted with a candle maker in Whinburg, and the result was a beautiful pillar candle scented with summer and flecked with dried flower petals, resting in a ring of silk leaves.

"I'm glad you've done this before," Hannah said when they

were finished, and surveying with pleasure their good work. "It looks beautiful, doesn't it?"

"It does," Cora said. "You're a fast learner—good thing, because we get to wash all those dishes and set up again, as soon as the first shift of a hundred and fifty have eaten." She grinned at Hannah's oh-my-goodness face. "Don't worry. We'll eat with the first group. The *Eck Leit* have to wait until everyone is finished."

Amanda's closest friends were these helpers in the wedding corner, and even now were carefully placing crystal glasses at each setting, nestling them in among curls of royal-blue ribbon. Amanda was using her wedding china, a pattern that Cora thought was pretty, but not to her own taste.

Then again, at least Amanda *had* china. The chances of Cora being able to choose anything at all—including a groom —for her own wedding were slim to none. She knew every boy in the Wet Mountain Valley, and while she had dated one or two, she'd soon concluded that even *der Herr* would shake His mighty head at her for not waiting patiently for Him to show her His choice.

There had been a time this past summer when she thought He'd done so.

How wrong she'd been.

She would not look for him. Instead, she bumped Hannah's shoulder with her own. "Come on, let's find a place to sit, before everyone comes in."

A second set of helpers brought out the bowls of hot food. Cora adored the traditional Amish wedding dinner. Broasted chicken was one of her favorite things in all the world, and she'd eat stuffing every day of the week if she could, instead of only on holidays and special occasions. Add to that mashed potatoes and gravy, homemade noodles, creamed celery, pepper slaw, and as many cakes, pies, and desserts as the women of the community could make ... bliss.

Now here came the wedding party, seated first, of course. Amanda glowed with happiness as she took the chair next to her husband. Their *Neuwesitzern* who had supported them during the wedding ceremony took their places next to them, while Isaac and Corinne Yoder, Sarah and *Englisch* Henry, and all Amanda's brothers and their families as well as Joshua's family filled the tables closest to the *Eck*.

Hannah glanced at her. "You're not going to look, are you?"

Hannah knew. She had come out west with Amanda and had witnessed Simon's behavior firsthand—and Cora's, too, afterward. In a strange way, it had brought the two young women closer together despite the fact that at the time, Hannah had been a lot more *Englisch* than she was now.

"*Neh*, why should I?" Cora hoped her voice sounded calm and unconcerned. "Amanda told me that his and Caleb's father was her oldest brother Michael. She always thought it was funny that her nephew is barely three years younger than she is."

"Her nephew who apparently has no name?"

"I must have forgotten it," Cora said pointedly. "And so should you."

Which of course was the moment she looked toward the family tables just in time to see Simon taking his seat next to his mother the *Dokterfraa*, and his gaze met hers.

As though she had been a bell struck with a mallet, a vibration rang through her.

Neh. Absolutely not. She would not allow him to have this effect on her again.

Mercifully, the bishop bowed his head and a sound like the wind in the pines rustled through the room as everyone stopped talking and bowed their heads in a silent grace. At the bishop's "Amen," a cacophony broke out as the wedding guests helped themselves to the food steaming in the bowls.

"How are you going to avoid him?" Hannah asked in a low voice, passing her the noodles.

"In case you hadn't noticed, we are in a tent stuffed to the brim with wedding guests," Cora replied. The noodles were superb. She spooned chicken on them and handed the bowl to Hannah. "I think I can manage it. But if I can't, I want you to help me. If he even looks in my direction, I want you to come over and talk to me. Even better, bring a boy with you."

"I don't know any of these boys," Hannah protested. "My folks are in Oak Hill, remember? Different *Gmee*."

"What do you *Englisch* girls do when you want to talk to a boy?"

"I'm less *Englisch* than I used to be," Hannah observed. "And I served them coffee at the shop or played multiplayer RPGs online. I don't think I actually talked to anyone much past 'one pump or two?'"

RPG, Cora remembered from when they worked together in Colorado, meant *role-playing game*. Which didn't leave her much the wiser, except that she knew it was played on a computer.

But enough of this. "Have you heard from Ben lately?"

Hannah lifted one shoulder. She was dressed Amish like Cora, in her best plum-colored dress, with a white Sunday cape and apron. The only differences were in Hannah's heart-shaped Lancaster County *Kapp* versus Cora's bucket-shaped Colorado one, and Cora's black cape and apron. But under her Amish clothes, Cora knew that a battle was going on in Hannah's heart. *Englisch* or Amish? Cora would never push her for a decision, because that was a sure way to send someone to the other side.

A lot of Hannah's hesitancy came from the fact that she cared about Ben Troyer. Cared whether he would choose the Amish or the *Englisch* life, too. Cora knew from experience how very easy it was to put your whole life on hold for a man, but what she still didn't know was why Hannah had come back from California alone. She could have stayed out there with Ben, or brought him back with her. But she'd found a third path that had brought her home.

"I hope you're the only one who asks me that today," Hannah mumbled around a mouthful of chicken. "What are the odds?"

"Not very good," Cora said, trying to be honest. "Everyone knows Bishop Daniel, and what happened, and that you and his son went to California."

Hannah groaned. "Can I leave now?"

"No. You have to help with the dishes. And the *Youngie* will all stay for supper, and games, and all kinds of fun. If it's the same here as it is in Colorado, you'll love it."

"Will you?"

"I'll be busy having fun and talking to boys I don't know. Of course I will."

"Can we stick together?" Hannah sounded anxious. "People might—you know—"

Ask me about Ben. Cora could hear the silent words. This was, after all, Ben's *Gmee*, and everyone in the township knew who Hannah was. The girl who had been kidnapped along with her sister when they were little. The girl who had grown up *Englisch* and was now learning how to live Amish while she decided which world she was going to live in.

"*Ja*, sure," Cora agreed. "You stick with me, and maybe by tonight we'll each have a boy ask to drive us home."

"In your dreams, girlfriend."

Hannah was smart enough to drop the subject, and Cora was perceptive enough to realize Hannah had not answered the question she was afraid everyone else would ask.

So she had not one but two pieces of pie, and coffee, and got to know the three sisters sitting across from them who ran the new bakery in Whinburg, and then it was time to clear the tables and do the dishes. A second set of tablecloths went down, and clean plates and cutlery, and this time the sage-green paper napkin went in the center of the plate with a curl of royal blue ribbon on it. There wasn't time to tie up the cutlery in bundles—hungry people were waiting—but they could still make the settings festive. Honestly, Amanda must have bought up every roll of narrow royal-blue ribbon in Lancaster County.

When grace had been said and everyone was digging in, she and Hannah had nothing to do until it was time to clear. Which was when she saw Simon making his slow but unmistakeable way along the aisles to where she and Hannah stood.

She grabbed Hannah's wrist. "Come on. Let's go talk to my cousin Mollie Graber. She's over there, against the wall of the tent. See her walker leaning on the post?"

"Sure, but—"

And when she reached Mollie's table, she leaned into her cousin's delighted hug just enough to glance back and see that Simon had gone.

2

Simon hadn't believed that Cora Swarey would actually come to Amanda's wedding.

He'd helped address the pile of invitation cards one evening when he and Caleb and Mamm and Englisch Henry were over at his *Mammi* and *Daadi*'s place, and thought then that sending one to Colorado was more for a keepsake than an actual invitation.

Luckily he hadn't said so out loud, because clearly he'd been wrong, which his little brother would have taken as a personal triumph and never let him forget it.

When he'd casually asked why they were sending an invitation out there, Amanda had said, "The Swareys have relatives here. And Cora and I became good friends working together at the Lost Creek Ranch. I saw a lot more of her and her sisters than I ever saw of you."

"I had work to do," he'd protested, and neglected to tell her that the reason he'd avoided the big house where the Amish girls worked as housekeeping staff and Amanda was assistant chef was because he was avoiding Cora.

Avoiding his guilty conscience.

Avoiding admitting to himself that he'd been an idiot, and thrown away his chance of happiness with both hands.

So the family had been staying here in Whinburg Township with Jeremiah Swarey, Cora's father's brother, and his family, and they might as well have been back in Colorado for all the chances he'd had to see her. Then, last night there'd been the accident during the sleighride, when Malinda Kanagy and Neil Wengerd had been upended into Willow Creek and nearly killed, which had sobered the *Youngie* of the township to the point where even going to singing was more like going to church. Cora had been at the sleighride, but he hadn't been able to talk to her then, either, what with the ambulance and all the excitement.

The days of the visit were running out. If he wasn't careful, she and her family would be back on the train before he was able to say a single word. Which was why, just before the wedding, he'd been driven to ask Amanda for her help.

She'd gazed at him in that way she had, that got under your skin and looked right into your heart. "Are you certain sure that's a *gut* idea, Simon?"

"*Ja*, I'm sure."

"Good for you, or for her?"

"For both of us, I hope. I'm not going to propose to her, Mandy. I just want to talk to her. To explain."

"I think she's probably tired of your actions doing all the talking."

Ouch.

"It wasn't how it looked. I was stupid. I know that now. I want to tell her that I've changed."

"Have you?" Amanda put down the pencil on her list with its two columns. Boys' names and girls' names. The bride's prerogative on her wedding day was to arrange the *Youngie* into couples to sit together at supper. "Did you know Cora joined church this past autumn? The old things are passed away. Don't you think you'd better leave the past in the past?"

His temper had bubbled up, then, and he'd almost turned and walked out of the house. But this was Amanda, who loved him in spite of his faults. And he loved her. Besides, he couldn't do this on his own. He needed her.

"Come on, Mandy, please?"

With a shake of her blond head, Amanda had picked up her pencil and drawn a line between their two names. "If she comes to me and says she never wants to speak to me again, I'm blaming you."

So here he was, socializing among the *Gmee* all afternoon as though he hadn't a care in the world, because he knew Cora would be sitting with him at supper. He saw her occasionally, stuck like glue to Hannah Riehl, whose brother Samuel even dropped in toward late afternoon. But the moment Simon approached, the two girls evaporated into the crowd.

"Hey, Sam," he greeted him, trying to look as though Sam had been his object all along. "Didn't expect to see you here."

Samuel looked behind him in a bemused fashion. "Did you just scare off my sister and Cora?"

"I hope not. Are you staying for supper?" Sam was dressed Amish, in a white Sunday shirt and black weskit like Simon's own, so maybe he planned on it.

"I was thinking about it. Amanda won't mind, will she?"

"She'd be happy if you did."

"I didn't feel right about coming to the wedding, but I did want to leave a gift and wish her well." He held a present wrapped in silver and white paper in his hands.

"They opened their gifts after lunch, but you can leave that in the house if you want. There's another pile growing on the dining room table."

"I'll do that."

Simon walked with him into the house, which was full of people warming up by the cozy woodstove in the kitchen. "Whew," he said when Sam had left his gift with the others and they were back outside, "it was hot in there."

"It's warming up. It'll snow before morning," Samuel said. "I'm glad she had sunshine for most of the day, even though it's cold. They're staying here tonight?"

Simon nodded. "They won't go far. Christmas with the family and then honeymoon visits around here so Joshua gets to know his new relatives in Lancaster County, and then they'll go back to Colorado around the end of January. When spring turkey season starts in April, he says, they'll be settled in and open for business at the butcher shop."

"Are you going with them?"

Simon blinked at him. "Why would I? There's no work out there in the winter. And I'm no butcher."

Samuel put his hands in his coat pockets to keep them warm. "Just wondered. What do you do for work here?"

Well, there was a sore spot. "Not much. Pick up odd jobs where I can. Help Henry in the pottery when I can't."

"I thought you were a buggy maker?" Samuel gazed at him from under his shaggy fringe and the brim of his black felt winter hat.

"I was, but— I um, got fired. Before I went to Colorado. That was one of the reasons me and Joe went."

"Oh. Sorry. Well, you could probably get work at the RV factory, where I used to work. They're always looking for help there."

Simon shook his head. "Not me. Didn't you tell me once how much you hated never seeing the sun?"

"*Ja*, but it pays better than the nothing you're probably making at the pottery."

Since when did Samuel get so smart? Time to turn this conversation around. "What about you? You're dressing Amish these days?"

"I'm back at home."

This was news. "You are? Since when?"

"Since Hannah came home from California."

November, then. Just around Thanksgiving. "So are you two tired of living *Englisch*? Going to join church?"

Samuel hunched his shoulders under his wool coat, as though he wasn't sure if it fit properly. "I don't know about her, but living *Englisch* is getting old. The *Ordnung* is hard, but somehow living with no rules at all is harder. I missed the family, and after all that stuff that went on at the ranch, it was just time to come home. Help Dat on the farm."

"He's happy to have your help, I bet."

"Yeah, he is. He'd be happier if I joined church, though."

"There's still time." When Samuel was silent, Simon took a shot in the dark. "You waiting for Hannah to make up her mind?"

The other young man eyed him. "How'd you come to that conclusion?"

Simon lifted a shoulder. "Seems natural. I can't imagine what you and she have been through, Sam. But if I had a sister and I wanted to stand by her, I might do the same. So she'd have someone on her side, whether she was in or out."

"Who are you and what have you done with Simon Yoder?"

It was meant to be a joke, so Simon grinned as though he got it. But when Samuel wandered off to find his sister again, he had to wonder. Why was life so easy for people like Amanda and so hard for people like him and Hannah and Sam? He'd joined church because that was the only way to get any peace, and he couldn't see himself living *Englisch*. But even he had to admit he wasn't very good at being Amish. On the outside, maybe, but not on the inside.

Never mind feeling sorry for yourself. It was nearly time for supper.

Time to put his plan into action.

BY SUPPERTIME, Simon estimated that about two thirds of the wedding guests had departed, leaving the newly married couples who hadn't yet started their families, couples who were going steady, the singles in the *Youngie,* and the bridal couple's families to eat supper together in the Yoders' big living room where they normally had the fellowship meal after church. The *Eck* had been recreated, beautifully decorated and already set with at least four layer cakes iced in white. But the place of honor was now for the bridal couple's parents. Isaac and Corinne Yoder and Wilmer and Savilla King shared it, along with Joshua's brothers and sisters, and Amanda's brothers and their wives. The house was warm and festive and smelled like the cinnamon sticks *Mammi* always used at Christmas, as familiar as his own home.

The perfect place to begin his courtship for real this time.

The single young men crowded into one of the upstairs bedrooms, the single women in the room opposite, which had been Amanda's. The eldest male helper of the *Eck Leit,* Joshua's brother Andrew, called out the names of one boy and one girl, the product of those columns on the bride's list.

"Simon Yoder and Cora Swarey."

Simon left the bedroom and met Cora at the top of the stairs. The look of outright horror on her pale face, though, nearly made him forget he was supposed to offer her his hand. For the first time, the thought flashed into his head that she might refuse to be paired with him—or worse, might already have made arrangements to sit with someone else regardless of the bride's list. His hand hung in the air for one frozen moment.

To his intense relief, she mastered the emotion on her face and placed her cold hand in his—the first time they had touched since that night six months ago when everything had fallen apart. Andrew King called the next couple's name as he and Cora descended the staircase in full view of everyone. Cora slipped into the seat next to him at the long table without a word.

He felt as though he had dodged a runaway mule. She was still as pale as a china plate.

"It's good to see you again, Cora," he offered. "I guess you're glad you're not a helper at this meal, anyway."

"It just means someone else has to do it," she said quietly. "I'm always glad to help, especially for Amanda."

Oh. Well. One setting was a lot of work. She'd done two. Three was too much, in his mind. Besides, it was good that the younger *Maedels* would learn how to serve.

Once as many of the girls and boys had been paired off as Amanda had arranged, they said grace. Simon passed Cora the macaroni and cheese, and made sure she had a nice slice of ham from the platter in front of them before he served himself. Peas, pickles, and his favorite home fries made of sweet potatoes made up the bulk of the meal, if you didn't count cold cuts, bread and jelly, and the array of desserts waiting on a side table. He knew for a fact one of those white cakes in the *Eck* was coconut snowball cake. Also his favorite.

But she didn't seem to be helping herself to as much food as he was. "Fries?" he offered. "These are great—Mamm makes the best. She says it's the paprika."

"I'm still full from lunch," Cora said. She took two sweet-potato fries and passed the bowl to the boy beside her.

Now that he'd managed to wrangle her this close after all these months, why couldn't he think of anything to say? "Your folks have gone?"

"Do you see them?"

He glanced around. "*Neh*—only your sisters."

"Then they've gone."

"You're staying with your uncle?" Of course he knew that. "*Ja.*"

"When are you all heading home to Colorado?" A long time from now, he hoped.

"Dat has to get back to the workshop," she said, not looking at him. She ate her macaroni and cheese two little elbows at a time. "Horses need harness no matter the season."

That didn't sound good. "After New Year's, then?"

"After Christmas. We'll stay for church, so Monday, I think. They had to call the *Englisch* taxi days in advance, it's so busy at this time of year."

"Monday?" he exclaimed. "*This* Monday?"

"That's what I said." She cut a tiny piece of ham. "Your listening skills don't seem to have improved since the summer."

His listening skills? "I heard you just fine. I just thought you'd be here longer. After coming such a long way, and family connections here."

She was related to Mollie Graber, who hadn't stayed for all

of the day's festivities, but had had to be taken home right after lunch. Mollie was a widow a little over thirty—Simon was vague on the details, but she'd lost her husband and young child in a buggy accident seven or eight years ago. Mamm was treating her for arthritis ... or was it an allergy? He didn't know what exactly was wrong with her, just that she had to use a walker.

"We've had a good visit," Cora told him, and laid her knife and fork down on her empty plate. "I'm going to see Mollie tomorrow."

He leaped on his opportunity like a sparrow on a seed. "Maybe I could drive you."

She stared at him. "My uncle's place is clear on the other side of Whinburg. Mollie lives in the basement suite of the Zucker girls' home. There's a bus stop next to the phone shanty at the end of his lane. Why wouldn't I just take the bus?"

"Why pay almost two dollars when you can ride with me for free?" He gave her his most charming grin.

But she didn't smile back. Instead, she turned her head, and he thought he heard her say, "Oh, it'd cost me."

But in the racket of people eating and talking, and his *Daadi* making jokes in the *Eck* and his family laughing, he couldn't be sure.

With every minute that passed, Simon was convinced the others at the table were watching him flop like a trout on the bank, completely unable to get any conversation going with Cora. She answered his questions with a polite *ja* or *neh*, no more. When he finally thought to ask open-ended questions, she found a way to talk to the people beside her, or across the table from them, drawing them into the conversation to get their opinions on his questions. Whether they thought the ice was going to hold on the pond for hockey. Whether they liked hot chocolate with marshmallows out by the fire after a game. Whether the newlyweds would escape their share of wedding pranks tonight, or if they'd find their new washing machine in someone's hayloft tomorrow, or all the sheets knotted together on the clothesline. And then she and Priscilla Mast got started on gardens, and he lost her for good—or at least until the helpers cleared the tables after dessert. And to add insult to injury, he'd been so focused on getting her to talk to him that the coconut snowball cake had been eaten right down to the plate and he didn't get so much as a crumb.

He had to change his strategy. If the Swareys were leaving on Monday, he didn't have much time to make Cora see that he cared. That he wanted them to be together. That he was serious this time.

Technically the bride's pairing-up of couples ended after dessert, but many stayed together, especially the ones who had put the bride up to giving them their choice.

Like him.

But not for the world would he tell Cora he'd done that. Let her think it was all Amanda, or God's will, the way bringing them together at the ranch had been. He hadn't realized it until it was too late, but he knew now. And now he was going to do his best to break down this wall she'd put up between them.

With the tables cleared, it was time for singing, and the song they'd begin with was the bride's choice. Simon thought Cora would like it if he helped to hand out the hymnbooks and song books, so he got up and joined his brother. He caught his mother's approving glance, since after all, as a member of the Yoder family such a task was appropriate for him and Caleb.

"I'd like us to sing my husband's choice," Amanda said in

her soft voice, her cheeks reddening as she said those words for what Simon thought might be the first time. "It's an old one—'Lord, Who at Cana's Wedding Feast'—and you'll find the words inside the *Gesangbuch* on a separate piece of paper. Cora, do you know the tune?"

From across the room, where he was passing out hymn-books, Simon could practically feel her body stiffen as her name was spoken. "Oh—Amanda, I don't think—"

"If ever there was a time to lift up our voices and make a joyful noise, *mei lieber freind*, it's today," Amanda said. "Say you know it. Please?"

"*Ja*, I know it, but I—I don't have a book," Cora said, clearly trying to find any excuse.

"Here." Simon slid the *Unpartheyisches Gesangbuch* in front of her, its brown cover already open to the slip of paper with the words neatly copied out.

"*Denki*," Cora whispered. She looked around to make sure everyone had a copy, and took a breath.

And then came the moment Simon hadn't realized he'd been waiting for. The moment when that first clear note rang out into the room.

Most of the *Youngie* hadn't heard her sing before, and it made them so *verhuddelt* they forgot to join in. But the Colorado *Youngie* chimed right in on the fourth note, just as they did at singing at home, supporting Cora as she led them through the first line at a respectable speed, the way they tended to sing the old *Englisch* hymns.

> Lord, who at Cana's wedding feast
> Didst as a Guest appear,
> Thou dearer far than earthly guest,
> Vouchsafe Thy presence here;

For holy Thou indeed dost prove
The marriage vow to be,
Proclaiming it a type of love
Between the Church and Thee.

This holy vow that man can make,
The golden thread in life,
The bond that none may dare to break,
That bindeth man and wife,
Which, blest by Thee, what e'er betide,
No evil shall destroy,
Through careworn days each care divides,
And doubles every joy.

On those who now before Thee kneel,
O Lord, Thy blessing pour,
That each may wake the other's zeal
To love Thee more and more;
Oh, grant them here in peace to live,
In purity and love,
And, this world leaving, to receive
A crown of life above.

A babble of excited conversation broke out when the hymn was finished, but before it could get out of hand, Joshua King spoke up.

"My wife's choice is page 323 in the *Unpartheyisches Gesangbuch*. Cora, could you start this one, too, please? Then maybe Noah can start the second three verses, and my brother Moses the last."

Most of the room had recovered themselves, and as they sang the familiar words, Simon could hear Cora's voice decreasing in power as she gave place to the unity of voices rather than simply leading everyone. It was what she had done in Colorado, too, the few times Simon had been able to go to church. It wasn't her way to draw attention to herself, even though God had given her an amazing gift. Simon had never understood it—why she should have been born into an Amish family when in any *Englisch* family she would have had singing lessons and maybe even some kind of career.

But there was no use in asking God why He did what He did. Every Amish child knew that the will of *der Herr* was to be obeyed, not questioned. His ways were as far above human ways as the sky was above the earth. Simon had learned long ago to keep his questions to himself. Sure, he had joined church. But that didn't mean he'd put his brain on a shelf and forgotten about it. It just meant he'd ask his questions silently and hope that someday, God would answer them.

After all, he'd prayed that he'd see Cora again, despite all the odds against it when they lived on opposite sides of the country. And here she was. The answer to his prayer.

Maybe even the answer to all of them.

3

A wedding was an all-day affair, and normally Cora would enjoy every minute. But today felt like an obstacle course, where traps yawned in front of her and she had to make a snap decision whether to jump or fall.

By eight o'clock she was exhausted at the mental effort it was taking to be within a hundred yards of Simon Yoder. She should have done what the spirit had prompted her to do, which was to drive her cousin Mollie home after lunch.

But she hadn't, and here she was, singing and making small talk with Simon and wishing she were anywhere but here.

"Are you all right?" Grace Ann, Amanda's new sister-in-law, bumped her shoulder companionably as they waited outside the bathroom. "This can't be easy."

"I wish I knew what was going on," she whispered back. "I refuse to believe that Amanda paired us up on purpose."

"She didn't." Grace Ann glanced over her shoulder, but no one was paying them any attention. "Simon put her up to it last night."

"But why?" Cora let out a long breath. "Why does he want to torture me like this?"

"Seems to me it would only be torture if you still had feelings for him," Grace Ann dropped her voice even further as someone passed them on the way to the back door. "You don't, do you?"

"*Neh*, of course not." But even as she said the words, she didn't know if they were true. Because honestly, she didn't know how she felt. Her emotions were whipping this way and that like a maple tree in a storm, and any moment her composure would tear away, leaving her exposed to the elements.

A few minutes in the bathroom alone was a gift, and she took the opportunity to pat her face with a cold cloth. She gazed into the small mirror above the sink and wondered who that stranger could be looking back at her. She looked familiar —reddish blond hair twisted up into her *Kapp*, a nose that would probably be beaky by the time she was fifty, an oval face. But the eyes of that girl had changed. Instead of being a sunny blue, ready to smile at anyone, they were shadowed and full of pain.

She couldn't go back out there like this. No wonder the people who knew her best were asking if she was all right. A couple more dabs with the damp cloth and she pasted on a smile, then took a deep breath and stepped out of the bathroom.

She practically collided with a man passing in the hall. Instinctively, his hand went to her elbow to steady her.

"I'm sorry, I didn't mean to bowl you over," he said, laughter in his voice. "You're Cora, aren't you—one of the *Youngie* from Colorado? Mollie Graber's cousin?"

The hallway was lit by the Coleman pole lamp near the door, so she got a good look at him. He had his coat and gloves on, his winter hat in the other hand, so he was clearly on his way home. He was tall, with curly dark hair and hazel eyes. Nice eyes. Freckles on his nose. Several years older than she, and clean shaven. It was unusual for a man over thirty to not be married. His hand was gentle, and it fell away, as though he didn't want her to think he was taking a liberty.

"*Ja,*" she said. "I'm Cora Swarey. Joshua and Amanda will be members of our church when they come back. Our family has been friends with the Kings for years."

"Dean Yutzy," he said. "I'm living with my *Onkel* and *Aendi* until I can afford a place—do you know Charlie and Amy Yutzy? They just leased a farm between Willow Creek and Whinburg."

"No, I don't," she said, "but it's nice to meet you."

She couldn't hide here in the hallway talking, though. Someone might see them and think they were flirting.

"Are your folks still here?" he asked.

"*Neh,* they left before supper."

"And Mollie? I—I wonder if you would think I was forward if I offered the two of you a ride? I have my own buggy. I was just going out to hitch up."

Goodness. This was more than flirting. Whether she and Mollie were cousins or not, this was taking *forward* to a whole new level. She'd known him for a grand total of two minutes!

He looked as though he knew it, too, and she half expected him to take back the offer. "That's very thoughtful, Dean, but Mollie went home after lunch. And I have a ride already."

His shoulders drooped a little in disappointment before he straightened again. "I might have known, a *Maedel* like you, with such a beautiful voice. A gift from God."

Oh my goodness, she didn't know which way to look.

"I don't want to embarrass you, but truly, it was a gift tonight to hear you."

"I—well, I—" Her tongue tangled in her mouth. *"Guder nacht."*

Cora practically dove into the downstairs bedroom to hunt up her coat and scarf, which she'd laid on the bed with a mountain of others. When she turned, there was Simon in the doorway. She clutched the warm coat to her chest so he wouldn't see the sudden pounding of her heart.

"Sure I can't drive you to your uncle's, Cora?"

What was happening tonight? Offers were pouring out of the sky. It must be wedding fever or something. For a moment she couldn't think who she'd made arrangements with when her parents had gone earlier. "I—I'm to go with the Zucker sisters."

"Tell them you got another ride. It's a bit out of their way."

By half a mile. Practically nothing. "But—"

"Please, Cora. I think we need to talk."

Now he wanted to talk? Now, not six months ago when she'd begged him to tell her what was wrong, why he was endangering his soul with his behavior, why—why—

Now?

He looked as if he was holding his breath, waiting for her answer. Well, she might as well go. Hear what he had to say. Forgive him again. Enjoy Christmas with a clear conscience. And then climb aboard the train Monday and forget him.

For good this time.

"All right," she said with a sigh. "I'll just let Amy Zucker know."

"Meet you in the lane."

So he didn't want the local *Youngie* to tease him about giving her a ride, did he? Well, it was perfectly fine by her if nobody knew he had asked her. Grace Ann would think she was crazy for going with him after she'd turned down a nice man like Dean Yutzy.

Maybe she wouldn't mention that, either.

A few minutes later she was walking down the left-hand track of the lane in her winter coat, scarf wrapped around her throat and her away bonnet keeping most of the cold off her ears. A buggy slowed, and Simon said, "Cora, it's me."

She hopped up on the bench next to him and slid the door closed.

"Here's a blanket." He handed her a folded woollen blanket and she spread it over her legs. "It's warming up. Sam Riehl says it'll snow before morning."

It didn't feel very warm. The blanket felt toasty in comparison. "Do you want some of this?" she asked.

"*Neh,* I'm fine. You double it over."

He turned out of the lane and on to the main road. If she remembered right, it was two miles to Whinburg, and half a mile or so past that to her uncle's. "So," she said. "You wanted to talk."

"Well, I hope you'll talk, too," he said in a self-deprecating way, which was unlike the cocky Simon she remembered.

"Why now, and not in the summer, when I wanted to know why you broke up with me?"

He was silent a moment, the jingle of the harness and the horse's hooves clip-clopping on the newly cleared road the only sounds. "I was ashamed. And it made me angry that people thought badly of me. I thought you were one of those people."

She didn't exactly roll her eyes, but she shook her head in disbelief. "Of course they thought badly of you. You flirted with an *Englisch* woman. A married woman. Your boss's wife!"

"It was only flirting," he said. "I never touched her, not even once."

"But she touched you."

"She—"

"People saw you, Simon. With her hand on your shoulder. Brushing back your hair. All of us—except maybe Amanda—knew about it. You were leading Mrs. Gunderson on like it was a game, and bringing shame on every Amish employee at the ranch with your behavior."

"It wasn't like that!"

"You go right ahead and think so," she told him, sitting straighter on the bench so there would be no accidental bumping of shoulders at a dip in the road. "You haven't changed one bit. Always trying to make yourself right after the fact, instead of simply doing the right thing in the first place."

He gave a sort of gasp, as if she'd winded him. Well, *gut*. He deserved to hear the truth. And she wasn't finished.

"We *Mauds* were just lucky that the ranch hands didn't assume we were as fast as you. It could have been really dangerous for us, especially when those *Englisch* started accusing the Amish men of poaching."

"But that was cleared up by the wildlife ranger."

"*Ja*, but it takes a lot more to clear up what people think of us—the *Gmee*. The reputation of the church came too close to disgrace. What if the Gundersons stopped buying from King Cuts and Meats? What if Mrs. Gunderson's friends in town boycotted the quilt store or the Fischers' market that's just getting off the ground? The churches aren't so big at home that they can exist without our *Englisch* neighbors, like they can here."

He shook the reins over the horse's back, though they were already going as fast as was sensible on a road that still had snow on it. "Is that really what you think of me? That I single-handedly could have destroyed the church in Amity?"

How like him to exaggerate his own importance. "Of course not. But it was visible, and you wouldn't stop, and it was just one more thing that would make people see us in a bad light."

"Well, it's good to know what you really think."

I'd have told you back in Colorado if you'd let me, and spared you this trip. No, she couldn't say that. That would just be mean. "You know what people thought. People tried to talk to you—Noah, for one. And Joshua. Don't act like this is all a surprise."

"It's a surprise to hear it from you." He hesitated. "I thought you might still care."

How had he thought that? Had it shown in her face? Oh, no, no. "I'm telling you what Jesus said—*if thy brother shall trespass against thee, go and tell him his fault between thee and him alone.* A person who tells another the truth shows they care, by being honest."

"Really?" He glanced at her. "Is that the reason? Because you do care? Cora, I really want that. I want us to be together, like we were this past summer."

Before she knew about Mrs. Gunderson. When they'd walked together in an alpine meadow in the sunshine, waist deep in blue and purple lupines, and he'd kissed her. When she'd thought, *I'll never be this happy again.*

She'd turned out to be right about that, at least.

"I told you why I'm saying this to you," she said steadily. "Because the Bible says I should."

"You forgot the rest of it, though," he said with another glance at her. "About forgiving seventy times seven."

Trust him to turn Scripture back on her! "Oh, I have forgiven you."

"I'm glad to hear it. But it doesn't sound like you've forgotten."

No, she hadn't. He was there in her heart, like a burr, no matter what she did to dislodge him.

But she was saved from a reply by the lights of her Onkel Jeremiah's place, so she directed Simon past the bus stop to the family's lane. Snow crunched under the wheels of the buggy as he turned the horse around in the yard. She folded the blanket and slid the door aside.

"Thank you for the ride."

"Thank you for the talk." He leaned over the seat as she jumped down. "I mean it, Cora. I know you haven't forgotten other things, too. Like how good we were together, you and me."

Maybe he remembered the lupines, too. But she only gazed at him, letting his words fall to the ground like snow. And just as unlikely to last.

She slid the door closed without answering.

As she climbed the front steps and let herself into the warm house, she heard him cluck to the horse and start up the lane. How very like him. *I thought you might still care. How good it was being together.*

How one-sided it was, listening to him. Last summer, when she was so in love, she'd never noticed how much of his conversation was about him in some way. And both then and now, not once had he said that he cared about her.

Which only went to show that he probably never had.

❧ 4 ❧

Ben Troyer
  1586 Live Oak Avenue
  Santa Cruz, California 95036

Dear Ben,

Merry Christmas! It was nice to get your postcard with your change of address. Didn't the carpentry job work out in San Luis Obispo? I looked on the map and saw that Santa Cruz was quite a ways north of there. Hope you were able to get the radiator fixed and the mighty Valiant made the trip OK.

It feels weird to write an actual letter and not type an email. But since my phone plan ran out and I'm not making any money to fill it up again, paper and pen it is. At least I don't need electricity to do this. The lamp works just fine. My sister Barbie and I cleaned all the glass chimneys this morning.

Amanda Yoder and Joshua King tied the knot this week. His uncles Simeon and Andrew were his side-sitters (I can't spell the Deitsch word), and Grace Ann and one of Amanda's cousins were hers. Did you know that Cora Swarey and her family came all the *way out here for the wedding? Amanda was so happy to have all her Colorado BFFs around her. Makes sense, I guess, if they're going to live in Amity. Plus which the Swareys have family in Whinburg.*

I'd never seen the custom of the bride putting couples together at supper. I would bet money that Simon put Amanda up to partnering him with Cora. What is he up to, I'd like to know? After the way he treated her? Maybe he's realizing that people are on to him, and he'd better get himself hooked up with someone before he's totally blacklisted. But Cora's too good for him. I hope she gives him the stone cold dumping he deserves.

In other news, you'll be happy to know that your sister Sallie got partnered up with one of the Zook twins (don't ask me which one—I can't tell them apart). Apparently she can, though, and they're adorable together. She sends her love, and wonders if you've learned to surf yet. I told her about that day in Long Beach, ha ha! I saw your mamm and the bishop but didn't get to speaking to them. Not a lot I can say anyhow, if you're still being hardheaded about writing. I don't want to blab your stuff if you don't want them to hear it.

I hope you're not mad at me for coming home without you. I mean, sleeping in the car is all right until we could find a cheap motel, but I didn't really want to do it for a steady gig, you know? And yes, I was a barista while you looked for work, but I just got so tired of feeling rootless. I did give it two months. That's something, right? Here I have an actual bed and can do something constructive and Mamm is so pathetically glad to have me home it makes me cry. Ashley (the sister formerly known as Leah) did great in her first semester at university so I'm pretty sure she's not going to come back to Oak Hill and join church. /understatement/

But I've been thinking about it. Church, I mean, not university.

Sam's here, too, did you know? He and I talk a lot. He's dressing Amish and helping Dad on the farm and so far they've managed not to butt heads like a pair of bellowing elk. Or bulls, or whatever animal it is that butts heads. It's funny how much he and I have in common. We could almost be siblings, ha ha. Both marking time here in Whinburg Township, wondering what we want out of life. What to do with ourselves. How much to commit.

Yikes, the c-word. I promised myself I wouldn't write it, and there I did. In pen, even. Never mind—one and done.

Take care of yourself—literally, like get some cream for those chilblains and eat a vegetable occasionally and buy a new pair of jeans if you're going to an interview.

I miss you.

Love, Hannah (the sister formerly known as Meghan)

❧

Cora counted herself lucky to get even a few hours of sleep, and this morning it had taken three cups of Aendi Kate's coffee to clear her brain enough that she could help with the housework. After lunch, she walked up the lane to catch the bus into Whinburg. It turned out she needn't have hurried—the bus was late. The snow Sam Riehl had predicted had come right on schedule, though, leaving six inches to cover up the snowplows' good work. And from the look of the grey sky, more would be on the way by the time she got back on the bus for her trip home.

She took careful steps up the walk to Mollie Graber's door. Some kind heart had shoveled it off—something Cora's mother always said would show you an optimist if ever there was one. Cora hadn't even got halfway to the door when it opened and there was her cousin, beaming as though they hadn't just seen each other yesterday.

"Aren't you a sight for sore eyes," she exclaimed. "Come on in—I've got some herbal tea on and some of the coconut snowball cake the Zucker girls made for Amanda's wedding supper."

Heaven. "I saw it in the *Eck* but of course it got cut first. How lovely they saved some for you."

Mollie made her slow way into her little sitting room using her walker and invited Cora to sit.

"Never mind," Cora said briskly. "I won't let you wait on me. You sit down right here and I'll bring everything in."

Mollie sighed with relief as she obeyed. "Mugs are in the cupboard to the right of the sink, and the cake knife in the drawer right below it."

Cora laughed. "We *must* be related. Mamm keeps those things in just the same places."

In no time at all they were seated together on the sofa and digging into fat slices of the cake, which was so light it practically floated, rich with coconut and a surprise layer of peppermint candy frosting between the three layers. Cora moaned with delight. "This is so good. I will stay here all winter and work for free if they'll give me this recipe."

She opened her eyes after her dramatic moment, expecting to find Mollie laughing. Instead, her cousin was gazing at her as though she'd been serious.

"Mollie? What is it? What did I say?"

Mollie rested her plate on her knees, which were covered with a beautiful Tulips quilt pieced in all the colors of spring. Another optimist must have made it, Cora thought.

"I wasn't going to bring it up right away ... but since ..."

Cora leaned forward and touched her hand. "Bring up what? Whatever it is, don't be shy. You can say anything to me, remember? We may be ten years apart in age, and a century apart in hard experience, but we've been friends as well as family all our lives."

Mollie nodded. "You're right. All I can do is ask, and all you can do is answer. So. The doctor says that while I might be falling apart, he thinks he can help. My knees are degenerating faster than they expected and I have to have both knee joints replaced. I'm to go in this afternoon for a pre-op visit, and then have the operation after Christmas, on Wednesday."

"Oh, Mollie," Cora breathed. So soon! "Both knees? But won't that mean that you—"

"Yes. It will be difficult. But the doctor feels that doing both at once is best. I'll be in hospital for three days, and then recovering at home for six weeks."

"Only six weeks?" That hardly seemed enough time for such serious surgery.

"Three weeks where I'd ... need the most help. Then three more weeks where he expects me to be more mobile. After that, only another six weeks or so before I'm as good as new."

And suddenly Cora put two and two together. "You want me to stay when my family goes home? And help you for those first three weeks?"

Mollie picked up her fork and cut a bite of cake, but didn't eat it. "As Mamm used to say, *I want doesn't get.* Usually. But I thought ... since we've always gotten along so well ... and it *is* winter and your mother might not need you so much ..."

Cora had already made up her mind. "Of course I'll stay."

Her cousin's eyes filled with tears. "You're sure? I could ask the girls upstairs to check in on me every day, but they're so busy with the business. Or I could ask my friend Anna Esch, but I have a feeling something is going to happen between her and that man who runs the buffalo ranch out your way ..."

Cora sat back in astonishment. "You mean Neil Wengerd?"

"*Ja.* I'm no prophet, but I predict we'll be hearing a little something about them in church pretty soon. So needless to say, I can hardly expect her to babysit me while he's here in town and she'll want to spend every moment she can with him."

"My goodness. There will be a disappointed *Maedel* or two if your prophecy comes true."

The twinkle was returning to Mollie's eyes. "But Anna has waited a lot longer for him than they have."

Cora laughed. "I want to hear that story for sure and certain. But for now we ought to—"

A thought struck her with such force it might as well have been a volleyball.

Three weeks. Maybe even six. Here. In Simon's church district.

"Cora, what is it? Is there something you need to do that has changed your mind? Because that's perfectly all right. Completely understandable."

What was he going to think? He'd probably leap to the assumption she'd wangled her way into her cousin's home just so she could warm up cold soup with him.

Not a chance in this world.

Cora made herself smile with as much reassurance as she could muster. "Nothing has changed my mind. Don't you worry."

"You went nearly as white as this cake for a second there." Mollie was looking honestly worried. "You must tell me, *Liewi*."

It would feel so good to confide in her. And knowing Mollie, she probably had a little idea about it, anyway.

"It's just that—well, I'm afraid people will talk. Dat has already said that we're going home on Monday. I was partnered with Simon Yoder for the wedding supper. Of all people. So if I stay, they'll think ... something got started again. Did you hear about what happened at the ranch where we were working last summer?"

Understanding dawned in Mollie's eyes. "I heard he got into some trouble, but nothing more. Did that trouble involve you?"

"No." Best not to say any more.

"Well, then. You honestly think people will say you're staying for his sake? They'll be able to see with their own eyes that's not true."

Cora shook her head so fast she had to reach up and reinsert one of the straight pins in her *Kapp*. "No. Not at all. But we did date. Out in Colorado. Briefly. I'm just afraid—*he* might think—"

"Not once he sees what you're doing for me, he won't. I'm such a demanding patient you won't have time to turn around, let alone go off riding in the buggy with him."

Mollie looked so stubborn and protective that Cora had to smile. "I'll need to ask my parents' permission to tend to my demanding patient."

"Of course you will. Once we have that, I'll put you in my second bedroom. I'm so glad I have one now—I almost didn't take this place because it seemed like too much space for one person." She took the bite of cake that had been waiting, and glanced at Cora. "I'm sorry about the trouble I'll be, but I'm not a bit sorry we get to spend some time together."

"You might find I'm pretty demanding myself." Smiling, Cora stood and picked up her plate. "There's one piece of cake left. I demand that we each have half to celebrate." From the kitchen, she called, "Are you coming to Onkel Jeremiah's for Christmas Eve?"

"Neh," Mollie said. "I'm invited to the Esches'."

"Christmas Day, then?" Cora came back in with the last piece of cake, and split it neatly between their two plates.

"*Ja,* but I need to call a taxi. Don't let me forget to do that before you go—the Zuckers have a telephone upstairs in the bakery and they gave me a key in case I need to use it."

"Nonsense," she said firmly. "It's hardly any distance at all. Dat and I will come and get you. One thing about our aunt and uncle's house—no matter how many people they fit into it, it's always big enough for more."

BY THE TIME Cora and her extended family walked into church on the Sunday after Christmas, everyone in Whinburg, Willow Creek, and all the way out to Oak Hill had heard that the girl who could sing so beautifully was staying to look after Mollie Graber while she recovered from double knee surgery. Dat had not hesitated to give his permission, and Mamm had nodded with approval. "I'll send a few more dresses and some of your things in the mail when we get home. Do you want that quilt you were working on?"

"Oh, that would be *wunderbar,*" Cora had said. "I only have the borders left, and those will take all of six weeks. Don't forget to send the bigger of the two hoops."

Church, as it happened, was at the home of the family next door to Englisch Henry and Sarah Byler. Thank goodness it wasn't actually at the Byler place, where Cora would have to spend the day devising ways to keep out of Simon's sight. But she must not have been as good at evasion as she thought, because his mother the *Dokterfraa* caught up to her in the kitchen after the fellowship meal.

"Cora, is it true, what I hear? That you're going to tend Mollie Graber after her surgery?"

"*Ja*, it's true," she said cautiously. She didn't know Simon's mother, really, and goodness knew what he had told her about them when he got home. Nothing, she hoped. He, after all, had not come out the hero in that story.

"Oh, good. I'm treating her for what the doctor thinks is arthritis, and what I think is a severe allergy to nightshade."

Cora blinked. "Nightshade? Is that a poison?"

Sarah shook her head. "Only to some people. She's not to have potatoes or tomatoes in any form, all right? And I agree with her doctor that she should avoid coffee, too. I have a salve for her hands that's quite effective for the stiffness, and a number of teas and cures that I think would help her knees in her recovery. Would it be all right to send them over sometime this week?"

"*Ja*, sure." Cora relaxed. "We have an *Englisch* taxi coming early Wednesday to take us to the hospital, and I'll go in it to pick her up again on Saturday night. But other than that, I should be at her place settling in, and moving things so she can reach them easily."

"*Ischt gut.*" Sarah smiled. "One of the boys will come over with a box, and every packet will have instructions with it so you'll know what to do. Mollie has an account with me, so no need to worry about having cash on hand."

Cora had lost track of every word that followed *One of the boys will come over*. She said something vague and Sarah went on her way completely unaware of the bombshell she'd just thrown. It seemed pretty certain that Simon had not confided in his family about their relationship, snipped off in the middle as it had been.

Dazedly, she located her family and stayed close to her

mother until they were ready to go home. No visiting for her, or singing later on, either. Luckily, when one or two of the girls asked, she was able to say that the family was leaving early in order to prepare for the train journey the next day.

It was the reverse of the trip they'd taken out here. First the *Englisch* taxi to the Lancaster station, then Lancaster to Pittsburgh, and Pittsburgh to Chicago. There, her family would transfer to the *Southwest Chief* and ride it all the way to Trinidad, Colorado, where another *Englisch* taxi would be waiting. Some forty-eight hours after hugging Cora good-bye, they'd be home.

And by then, Mollie would be home, too, and Cora would be so busy that she wouldn't have time to think about Simon Yoder.

Out of sight, out of mind.

Hannah Riehl
   2713 County Line 3
   Oak Hill, PA

Dear Hannah,

Thanks for your letter. It was the only thing I've received here so it was kind of a surprise. I haven't been in Santa Cruz long enough to run up any bills. You'll be happy to know I'm living in an old Airstream trailer behind an artist's house, so I have a real bed. If you hadn't lost your patience we could have been here together. It's warm compared to Pennsylvania, and while it does rain, when it's sunny it's amazing. I'm going to learn to surf as soon as I can afford a used board and a wetsuit. They surf here all year round. The Valiant could use some new tires and a radiator, though, so probably that will have to come first.

Until I get some paying work, I'm clearing this property in lieu of rent. More like logging it. I don't think a human has set foot back here since the sixties, when this place was some kind of religious commune. The artist is loaded. He doesn't need rent or to sell paintings, which I *guess is lucky for me. Once I get done with the property I'm going to start fixing things up in the shop and making them work again. It could take me a year. But he pays me enough to buy groceries so at least I don't have to shoot squirrels and dig ancient potatoes out of this old garden for my supper.*

Thanks for the local news. You can tell Sam hi from me. I don't expect I'll see him again if he joins church. I'm planning to make my life out here now. Sounds like you're settling in at home. I sort of expected it, but hoped you'd change your mind. Can't really see you getting married and raising a batch of kids though. You'd be teaching them Minecraft on your forbidden phone, ha ha.

If you do decide to come back this way, this address should be good for a few months.

I miss you, too.

Ben

❧

"Be careful with your horse," Mamm told Simon as she lifted her box of cures on to the seat beside him on Thursday. "It's New Year's Eve, and some of the *Englisch* may have started celebrating early. There will be lots of traffic."

"I will, Mamm," Simon said as soothingly as his impatience would let him. "Any message for Cora and Mollie?"

"*Neh*, Mollie's heard all my lectures, and all Cora needs to know is inside each packet." She smiled at him through the door. "But you can give them both our greetings, and let them know that if they need anything, to just say so and we'll see that they have it."

She slid the buggy door shut, and Simon clicked his tongue to Comet, his gelding. Caleb had wanted to run this errand, but Simon had overridden him. Along with this handy excuse to see Cora, he had a stop or two to make along the way.

The roads were not as slippery as Mamm feared, but they were enough to make him moderate his normal spanking pace. Sending his relatively new buggy into the ditch and hurting poor Comet into the bargain was not on today's agenda.

Looking for work and seeing Cora were.

He started with Whinburg Pallet and Crate, which used to be run by Amelia Beiler, but had been taken over by her second husband, Eli Fischer, so that she could go back to managing her home and family.

"I don't have any jobs open just now, Simon," Eli said, pushing up his hat with one finger after Simon had inquired. Around them, the shop seemed to be pretty busy, and since the Amish didn't typically celebrate the *Englisch* New Year's Eve much—for them, the new year began at Christmas, with Christ's birth—the men were still at work. One guy worked the air nailer while another helped a truck driver stack pallets on a flatbed. "We're a pretty small outfit. What kind of experience have you got?"

"I was with Oran Yost, the buggy maker, but it didn't work out. Do you know of anything else in town?"

Eli thought for a moment. "You might try the scratch and dent. They were looking for someone in the back, last I heard."

"In the back? Like the back of the store?"

Eli nodded. "Receiving crates and pallets of goods, getting them off the trucks. I don't know what they pay, but you'd build a good set of muscles, anyhow."

The Pequot Grocery, known to the Amish as the scratch and dent, was a little out of his way, but it was worth a try. Jobs were hard to come by in the township, but he didn't want to go out to the RV factory, where Sam Riehl and Ben Troyer used to work. If he wanted Cora to stick around after Mollie was better, he'd better settle down to something and show her he meant business. Meant to be the kind of man she could trust for the long haul. Granted, unloading stuff that had a little shipping damage, or didn't quite meet the standards of the *Englisch* grocery stores, was pretty humble work. But at least it was work.

But when he got there and located the manager in the rear of the store, marking quantities on the shelf against a list on a clipboard, the woman shook her head. "I'm so sorry, Simon. We just hired one of the Byler boys into the job yesterday."

Simon swallowed his disappointment and reflected that the store was, after all, a little out of the way. "*Denki*, Frannie. If you hear of anything else coming open, maybe you could let me know."

She paused for a minute, looking thoughtful. "As a matter of fact, I did hear about something. I think Kelvin Zook might need another pair of hands. Dean Yutzy is working there, but business at the smithy has been pretty good and Kelvin was hoping to get more help."

The smithy? Simon's heart sank. Working at the buggy shop had been hard enough, and working as Oran Yost's apprentice even harder. They had not got along, and Kelvin Zook was made in the same taciturn mold, only younger. The smithy was hot, hard, skilled labor. Granted, horses had to be shod, and there were a lot of horses in Lancaster County, but still ... it was not the work Simon had envisioned for himself.

Not that he'd spent a lot of time working or even envisioning it. But desperate times called for desperate measures, and time was in short supply.

So here he was, pulling up in front of a sign that said

ADINA SENFT

Whinburg Smith & Farrier in wrought iron at the gate. The shop occupied a quarter acre or so beside an auto repair outfit. In the yard, Simon tied Comet to a rail that had clearly been made right there in the shop. The business was in a big shed, with the Zook home on the adjoining property to the rear. The sound of hammers striking metal came from inside. His prospective employer, at least, was home.

Kelvin Zook lifted his head as Simon walked in. A figure in the back whom Simon took to be Dean kept up his work on a horseshoe, maintaining a regular, clanging rhythm. The shop was warm and unconsciously, his body relaxed. Though he had to wonder what it would be like in here in August.

"Help you?" Kelvin asked. "It's Simon Yoder, *nix*?"

"*Ja*, it is. I heard you might be looking for some more help."

Kelvin put down his hammer and tilted his head toward the yard. "Put your horse in the barn and we'll talk a bit."

Simon did so, for there was no grazing for Comet in the snowy yard, and the smith was evidently a hospitable man, for there was a flake of hay in the warm, three-stall barn. Then he returned to the smithy, still not convinced this would be the place for him.

Kelvin looked him up and down. "You had any experience bending iron?"

Simon shook his head. "Only to bring a horse here to be shod once or twice. I was apprenticed to Oran Yost, but—" *The truth will set you free.* "But he let me go. Didn't like me questioning and talking back."

"Can't say I would, either. Though I did plenty of it as a younger man."

"Guess I'm still growing out of that, then." Simon's smile was rueful. "But if a man has an idea he thinks might work,

46

and speaks up, at least the other fellow might listen, even if he decides against it in the end."

"Buggy-making is a trade that doesn't really allow for new ideas," Kelvin pointed out, leaning a hip on his workbench. "Smithing, too, to some extent. Can't get too fancy with horseshoes."

"But you make more than horseshoes, *nix*? Like that hitching rail out front. And I saw a gate on an *Englisch* place on the county road that looked like it might have come from your shop. It had birds on it."

"That was ours," Kelvin acknowledged. "I never made a bird before, but the lady of the house was dead set on blackbirds on the gate. Blackbird Farm, they call it."

"They were good birds," Simon said. "What else do you make?"

"Plain gates—just rails and bars, enough to keep the cattle in. Tools. Crowbars. We do a pretty good trade in that kind of thing."

"What about household stuff?" Simon asked, thinking of things he'd seen that might be converted to wrought iron. "Towel racks, mug trees, decorative hinges, that kind of stuff?"

"Hinges, we do," Kelvin allowed. "For barns. Not kitchen cupboards."

"The *Englisch* like them. Some can get pretty fanciful, mind you."

"We don't really cater to the *Englisch*," Kelvin said, prodding the bar he was working on. "Amish working men, mostly."

Simon had a flash of inspiration. "If you take me on, maybe I could try a few things like that, see how they do? Not things just for the *Englisch*, but things our sisters might like, too. Practical things. Coat hooks, drawer pulls, plus what I said before."

Kelvin was frowning now. "Those are small pieces. They'd just get in the way around here."

"Not if it was me making them and selling them. My mother has a stall in the Amish Market. I could ask her if I could have some space on Saturdays and see what I could sell."

Kelvin held up a hand. "That's putting the wagon before the horse. I ain't even said I'd take you on and train you, and already you're selling stuff in the Amish Market?"

"It's good to plan ahead," Simon said with a grin.

The other man nodded. "I can see why Oran Yost had a problem with you."

Simon's self-confidence deflated, and so did his enthusiasm for the job. Served him right for getting excited in the heat of the moment. He'd forgotten Kelvin's reputation.

"Well," he said, "*denkes* for your time. I'll not keep you from your work." He turned away, noticing as he did so that the ringing sounds had ceased. The other man at the back had finished with the horseshoe and was watching them. Dean Yutzy. Simon had seen him talking with Cora at the wedding supper. He nodded at the man, who nodded back.

"Not so hasty, Simon Yoder."

In surprise, he turned back to Kelvin.

"I haven't said my piece yet. Who's interviewing who, here?"

Simon had to acknowledge the man was right. "Sorry. You are, of course."

"You can admit you're wrong. That's a good sign. It takes some years to master iron, but I'm willing to start you out small. Hoof picks. Bars. You do all right with those and we'll talk again about towel racks and suchlike. I can see that such things would be *gut* time fillers in between major orders and the regular farrier business."

"You mean you're willing to hire me?"

"*Ja*, I said so, didn't I? But mind—I'll not have talking back and insolence. Smithing is hard work, and a moment of hard-headedness or not following safety rules can lose you an arm— or your life. *Verschteh?*"

"*Ja.*"

"I appreciate the difference between a good idea and a man getting above himself. Maybe Oran thinks they're the same. But he's boss in his own shop, and I'm boss in mine. You remember that and we'll get along well. All right?"

"*Ja. Denki.*" Simon could hardly believe it. "When can I start?"

"Monday too soon for you?"

"Not at all."

"*Gut.* We open at seven, close at five. When you've shown me you can be trusted on your own, you and Dean there can split shifts if you want. Long as at least one man is here with me all the time, I don't much care who it is. It's not safe to work alone." He named a wage that seemed more than fair to Simon during his training, with the possibility of raises once he'd learned his way around. And it was done.

He backed Comet out of the barn and rolled the door shut, feeling a little dazed at his success. He climbed into the buggy and clucked to the horse. *Der Herr* had been guiding him for sure and certain today. If he'd gone to see Cora first, as he'd originally wanted, he'd have made a poor showing of it. Now, he could approach her as a workman worthy of his hire, a man who could eventually support a wife and family.

Maybe Dean Yutzy was that kind of man, too. But Simon would guess that Yutzy hadn't run a few good ideas past Kelvin Zook and gained his reluctant approval.

This day was certainly looking up. And when Cora realized

he'd not only come all this way to bring her cousin the cures Mamm thought would help her, but had also landed paying work, Simon would look into her eyes and ask her if he might come courting for serious this time.

❧

"MOLLIIEEE," Amy Zucker called down the stairwell to the downstairs suite. "You've got companyyyyyyy."

"A young man," her sister Dora added, a giggle in her voice.

"*Denki,*" Mollie called up the stairwell as she hobbled past it on Cora's arm. "But in that case, it will be for Cora."

"Nonsense," Cora said to Mollie. "Five more steps and you can sit at the kitchen table."

"You're so bossy, young lady," Mollie groaned, releasing Cora and sinking into the chair. "I hope he turns out to be a door-to-door salesman, just for that."

But it wasn't, not this late in the day. It was Simon Yoder, carrying a cardboard box full of packets and bags. "*Guder owed,*" he said. "I brought Mamm's cures for Mollie."

Of course she couldn't take the box, say *denki,* and close the door in his face after he'd come all this way. So she held the door for him while he stepped past her, bringing a wave of cold with him.

"Brrr," she said. "Let me take that while you wipe your boots."

She carried the box into the little kitchen, where she found Mollie up, one hand clinging to the counter while with the other she poured hot tea from a familiar-looking packet into three waiting mugs. "Mollie Graber, *was tut dich?* You sit down."

"A few minutes standing every day, the doctor said," her

cousin reminded her with a twinkle. "Can't let Simon go without a hot cup of something after driving from Willow Creek." She spooned honey into the tea. "And maybe nip upstairs to see if Amy can spare a couple of her red velvet cupcakes. She made them especially for Christmas."

"I'll go," Simon said, coming into the kitchen.

Before either of them could reply, he'd loped up the steps, where greetings and giggles told Cora he'd surprised the girls in the back of the bakery. She rolled her eyes. "Now it will be twenty minutes before we see those cupcakes, if we see them at all. He is the worst flirt."

But the words were barely out of her mouth when boots came back down the steps and there was Simon, carrying a much smaller box—a pink one this time. "The girls say these are a belated Christmas present, since they didn't see you on Christmas Day."

"How kind they are," Mollie said. "Help yourself while Cora brings your tea. Are you going to tell me what all your *mamm* sent?"

"She says the instructions are in each packet," he said through a bite of red velvet cupcake. "This is really *gut*."

"Those girls have a gift with flour and sugar," Cora said. "Lucky for us it was the *gut Gottes Wille* for them to open a bakery, because all three have a talent for it. I can bake bread and made a pretty respectable birthday cake, but nothing like this." She closed her eyes as the rich flavor of the cupcake filled her mouth. "Mm."

When she opened them the next second, it was to find Simon gazing at her with such intensity it was a wonder her skin didn't burn.

Maybe it was. Because she was blushing.

Argh!

"How are you recovering, Mollie?" he said, turning to her cousin as though nothing had happened.

Mollie, it was clear, knew perfectly well that something had just happened. But thank goodness she was not the kind of woman who would say so. At the moment, at least. "I'm doing very well, I think," she said. "You can tell your mamm that between depriving me of mashed potatoes and spaghetti sauce and coating me in salve, I'm beginning to get my flexibility back. As for the knees, I'm to walk a certain number of minutes every day, and sit with my knees elevated if I have to sit. It would be easier just to stay in bed, but…"

"But not only would that be boring for both of us, it would also hinder the healing process," Cora finished. "By the end of three weeks, she'll be able to walk around without help, and she'll never want to see this nagging cousin of hers for the rest of her life."

Both of them laughed.

"And you, Simon?" Mollie asked. "Your family are well?"

"*Ja*, very well, now that the wedding is over and things can get back to normal. Mammi and Daadi are talking about going to Pinecraft in February, maybe, if Amanda and Josh will go with them. Both my great aunts live there, and their families are planning to go. The newlyweds could see them all at once."

"That will be a *wunderbaar* trip if it comes off," Cora said. "I've never been to Florida, but I hear it's beautiful, and the churches in Pinecraft are very welcoming."

"And I have some news of my own." Simon looked as though he was about to burst with it. "Kelvin Zook at the smithy is taking me on, starting Monday."

Cora sat back, trying not to stare. "You're going to be a blacksmith?"

His gaze dropped a little. "Is that such a surprise?"

"*Neh*," she said hastily, realizing how that might have sounded. "I thought you might prefer working in a shop, or making furniture, like the Millers do."

"The smithy makes gates and shoes horses, don't they?" Mollie asked. "Dean Yutzy works there, too, though I believe he has some experience. He just moved back here from Mifflin County around Thanksgiving, I think."

Cora willed herself not to blush at Mollie's casually informative tone. "Did he? Kelvin will have his hands full teaching two new men their work, then."

"He seemed to like my ideas," Simon said. "I thought the shop might branch out into household items. Smaller things that I could make to bring in a different kind of customer. Less seasonal."

"Like what?" What household items were made in a blacksmith shop?

"Like that." He pointed at the plastic paper towel holder. "The coat rack by the door could have wrought-iron hooks. The pull knobs on your cupboards could be little twists of iron."

"Quilt racks," said Mollie, nodding. "Especially the kind the *Englisch* like, to hang the quilts on the wall to look at instead of using them on a bed."

"I hadn't thought of that, but you're right," Simon said. "Maybe if I make one, Evie Troyer would display one of her quilts on it in her stall at the Amish Market."

"Aren't you full of ideas." Cora hoped she didn't sound patronizing, but supportive. Though she couldn't see Simon as a smith at all. He was the kind of man who would be good behind a counter at the Amish Market, or writing up orders in a shop. But then, he'd wrangled horses on the pack trips at the

Lost Creek dude ranch, hadn't he? It had been hard physical labor, too.

"How long does it take to learn to be a blacksmith?" Mollie asked. "Kelvin has been at it since he was a boy, and learned his trade with his father before the accident."

"A few years, I think," Simon said. "I don't expect to be twisting iron for towel racks tomorrow. Kelvin is going to start me on hoof picks and crowbars. But it's *gut* to come to a trade with ideas, *nix*?"

"*Ja*, it is," Cora said. "I hope you will do well."

"You don't sound certain."

She lifted a shoulder. "You're a man, and in charge of whether you do well at your trade or not. The point is to have *gut* work to do, and as the Bible says, *whatsoever ye do, do it heartily, as to the Lord, and not unto men.*"

"It sounds like you're singing it."

She looked down into her mug. "I may have made a little song about that once, back home."

"Do you remember it?"

He looked honestly curious, so she sang a few bars properly. A smile spread across his face. "That's a beautiful song. And a beautiful singer."

And just like that, all the warmth she'd felt at hearing he was settling to good, honest work evaporated. "Don't."

"Don't what? I'm just telling the truth. It's a beauti—"

"I heard you the first time, Simon. Don't pay me compliments when you can't be truthful." She held up a hand before he repeated himself. "I am not beautiful, nor do I want to be. I am as *Gott* made me, and if you have to give a compliment, give it to Him."

"Don't be so hard to please, Cora." She'd nettled him now.

Well, serve him right for thinking she was so shallow as to lap up his silly compliments the way a cat lapped milk.

"You don't need to please me," she said stiffly. "You need to please *der Herr*. And now if you've finished your tea, we'll say *denkes* to your *mamm* for sending along the box, and see you on your way. Mollie has another set of exercises to do—" Her cousin opened her mouth, and at Cora's glance, shut it again. "—and we need to get started."

Simon downed the last of his tea. "All right. Thanks for the tea, Mollie. See you soon, Cora." Instead of leaving his cup on the table, he took it to the sink, and then pulled on his coat and went out.

Mollie was silent until they heard the sound of his horse's hooves on the short asphalt drive, then the regular clip-clop as he turned on to the street. As the sound faded, she turned a thoughtful gaze on Cora.

Who got up and took the remaining dishes to the sink.

"He's still sweet on you, that boy," Mollie said.

"He thinks he is. But I also know him too well to believe it, or to still be sweet on him in return."

"But you were. Back in the summer."

"I was," she admitted. "The good thing is, I can learn a lesson so well that I don't need to be taught it twice."

"I see." Mollie put her hands on the table and levered herself to her feet. "Well, so I don't make a liar out of you, let's get busy with those exercises. He'll be back, you know."

But Cora was already getting the floor mat and the pillow ready, and pretended not to hear.

❧ 6 ❧

New Year's Day just happened to fall on a Friday, and a singing and supper were to be held at Paul and Barbara Byler's, the parents of the twins Jake and Joe. Mollie insisted that Cora go.

"I'll be fine on my own for one evening. I'm going to read this nice fat historical novel I've been hoarding just for my recovery, and you're going in the buggy with the Zucker girls."

Since it was fruitless to argue, and Cora hadn't been out of the house in a week except to fetch a few groceries, she went. The Zuckers were good company, and by the time they arrived at the Byler place and handed the horse and buggy off to one of the young hostlers, her stomach hurt from laughing and the sky had cleared just enough for the last of the sun to shine on them as they crossed the snowy yard.

Cora had met many of the *Youngie* at Amanda and Joshua's wedding. Still, it was strange not to see her and Joshua there, or Noah, or any of her other friends. They'd be home by now. Cora stifled a pang of homesickness as she laid her coat on the downstairs bed. This was the longest she'd been away from her family. Not that Mollie wasn't family. But it felt strange to be without her sisters and Mamm—something she hadn't anticipated when she'd leaped at Mollie's invitation.

The Zucker sisters, on the other hand, could nearly always be found together in a group, like ducks, swimming about and making a joyful noise unto the Lord. What would happen when one of them got married? Would she still work at the bakery, or stay home to keep house for her husband? Could the other two manage the bakery without her? And what of the sister's gift for baking? Of course her husband and family would be the beneficiary of that, but would it be like hiding her light under a bushel?

Cora shook her thoughts away. Nothing like imagining out a whole life for people she barely knew.

"Cora," said a voice beside her. *"Wie geht's?"*

She looked up, startled. "Dean ... Yutzy, isn't it?"

He looked pleased. "You remembered."

"It's hard to forget a man who asks to take you home the first time he speaks to you," she reminded him dryly.

"I hope you don't think I do that all the time. It was just that I had heard you were leaving and there you were, and so I asked."

"As you can see, I didn't leave. I'm helping my cousin while she recovers from knee surgery."

"Neh, I meant—" He stopped. "I'm sure Mollie appreciates you. Watch out for the third week, when the patient is convinced they're well and can manage on their own. It's then that accidents can happen and set them back."

Cora gazed at him in surprise. "You sound as though you've had some experience."

"My *Daadi*. I stayed in the *Daadi Haus* with him when he had a knee replacement and was foolish enough to listen when he said he was well enough to manage and I could go back to the house. I was only a boy of twelve, and obeyed my grandfather." He shook his head. "It was a lucky thing that Mamm just happened to go over with a plate of cookies she'd made, and found him on the floor unable to get up. A trip to the doctor and a stern lecture later, I was back in the *Daadi Haus* ... and for an extra week, to boot."

"My goodness. I'll be sure to tell Mollie to take that to heart. I would hate for her to be hurt—she's had so much pain to bear already."

"She has." For a moment, he looked as though he had had a pain or two to bear himself, and could sympathize. He glanced at the Zucker sisters across the room, laughing with a group of *Youngie*. "All of you are here—is she all alone?"

"By her own wish. Or maybe I should say her own command. But I left her tucked up in bed with a book, and she promised not to move unless it was necessary, and she'd use her walker."

"Do you think that was wise?" he asked. "To leave her alone so soon after surgery?"

"I don't know how well you know Mollie," Cora said, "but if I'd tried to stay, I'd have found my coat on despite myself and the business end of her cane prodding me out the door."

"I can't say I do know her," he admitted. "Now, anyway."

Cora recalled that Mollie had said he'd moved "back" from Mifflin County. "Did you live here in Whinburg Township before?"

"Yes, until I was about sixteen. When we moved after Dat died, I apprenticed to a blacksmith. It was sheer luck that Kelvin Zook had just lost his two helpers this past fall, and needed another man when I found myself back here."

"I hear Simon Yoder is starting there on Monday as well."

"*Ja*, he came by to talk with Kelvin yesterday. If he's not going to apprentice with Kelvin, I suppose his training will fall to me."

"Good luck," Cora said with what she felt was admirable restraint.

"Why do you say it like that? He presented himself well, I thought."

"No, I meant it," Cora said hastily. "He seems very happy to be starting work there. He has all kinds of ideas for things to make. He told us all about it."

"Oh, he did?" Dean seemed to draw back into himself. "He came over to Mollie's?"

"*Ja*, yesterday, probably as soon as he left your shop. His mother is the *Dokterfraa* here, and she sent a box of cures with him."

"Oh, I see." He seemed to relax, then stiffened up again. "You all must be good friends."

"Well, Mollie has known him since he was a baby, of course. I only met him last summer, when he was working in our district in Colorado." And that was all anyone here needed to know. Especially kind men with nice eyes. She nodded toward the tables set up in the Bylers' spacious living room. "They're setting out the books. Time to sit down, I think."

"Nice getting to know you, Cora." Dean smiled and then slipped away to find a place among the older young men, where he was warmly welcomed.

As Cora took her own place with the Zucker girls, it occurred to her that they hadn't really got to know one another. How could they, in all this crowd? And anyway, they'd talked mostly about Mollie and Simon, not themselves. Oh well, what did it matter? In a few weeks she'd be getting ready to go home.

What could happen in that short a time?

Nothing of a lasting nature, that was for sure.

Joe Byler, who was acting as host this evening, waved the last of the *Youngie* into their seats. "We'll start with 'How Great Thou Art.'" With hardly a pause, he sang the first note and on the second, everyone joined in. Cora was halfway through the first line when she realized a few brave souls were singing in parts—something they did in Colorado but which she had always thought wasn't done here. And who was that singing tenor to Dean Yutzy's bass? Could that be Simon?

She hadn't realized he even knew how. She reined in her galloping thoughts and concentrated on the grand old verses.

When the hymn came to a close, Joe said, "Cora Swarey, maybe you would be our *Vorsinger* and choose the next song?"

My goodness! Do they have no one to ask that they have to settle for me? Then Cora recovered herself. It was because she was a guest. They were making her feel welcome and included, that was all. She raised her voice and gave the number in the *Liedersammlung* for *"Nun danket alle Gott,"* one of her favorites.

After that, thank goodness, Joe's brother Jake chose one and started it, and then for half a dozen songs they alternated between boy and girl *Vorsingers*. It was different in Colorado, probably because there were only two or three dozen *Youngie*, and she was usually *Vorsinger*. But it seemed to her that the *Youngie* here had it right. Why should only one person have the privilege? When she got home, she'd simply invite someone else to choose a hymn, and after the initial shock, maybe they would become used to it. After all, their deacon was in his eighties and wasn't going to be around forever. Someone would have to begin the hymns in church, and since it couldn't be her, when better than now to get some of their young men used to doing it?

After an hour, they broke for supper, when the *Youngie* could sit in groups, or a boy could sit with a girl if he thought he would be welcome.

Strange how she could hear Simon's voice through all the hubbub of visiting and laughing. He had a nice voice. What a shame her most vivid memory of it was, *I don't think we're meant to be together, Cora.*

I don't think. Not *I've been praying for God to show me His will.* Not *What is God saying to your heart, Cora?* But *I.* With Simon, it was always *I.*

"I hope this seat isn't taken?"

With a start, she realized Dean Yutzy was once again standing there, only this time with a plate of food in his hand. In the other was a selection of cookies and cake.

"Neh," she said. "Are you going to eat that whole plate of sweets yourself?"

He chuckled as he slid into the place next to her. "I confess I was hoping we might sit together. I brought some of everything, because I don't know what you like."

"Let's eat our dinner, and then I'll tell you. But don't you dare touch that cherry slice."

Smiling, he dug into his plate of food. The Bylers had dished up a feast for this first day of the new year. Cheese melted in creamy macaroni, green beans crunched with baked noodle topping, and there was a big tureen of chicken and dumpling stew to warm everyone up just in case singing hadn't done so.

"You were saying you lived here before," Cora said, savoring a fluffy dumpling a bite at a time. She wished she could make them like this. "Did you know Mollie then, before she was married?"

Dean nodded, then swallowed so he could speak. "When

we were children, mostly. Our district split, so I didn't see her in church, but the *Youngie* carried on as though the split hadn't even happened, of course. She started having problems with her knees when we were about fourteen. Then when I was sixteen, as I said, we moved away and I didn't hear much more of her other than that she was married. And then the accident, of course. God's will can sometimes be very hard to bear." He was silent a moment, then seemed to recover with a visible effort. "I'm glad she had the operation. A little pain and inconvenience now, but the reward will be freedom."

"Like your *Daadi*," Cora suggested.

"Not like my *Daadi* at all." Cora was a little taken aback, but then he smiled and said, "Unlike him, Mollie was a grasshopper. Always doing, always organizing the *Youngie* and thinking up jamborees for us, like caroling at the assisted living center at Christmas, or helping at the mud sales for the volunteer fire crew."

This was so unlike the woman she was now that Cora was intrigued. "Do you really think she can have that life again?" Then she corrected herself. "Of course she can, if anyone can."

"You're right there," Dean said, nodding. "The next time you visit, maybe things will be different. Maybe she'll be married with a *Boppli* on the way."

"That *would* be different. But it's the rare man who can see past the walker to the woman she really is. And I believe I might think less of anyone who came courting once the walker was gone when he wouldn't when it was there."

Dean concentrated on his dinner. Then he said, "Tell me about the church in Colorado. Are you in Westcliffe?"

"No, we live in a little town called Amity a few miles north of there. There are about fifteen families, and since the growing season is so short, most have businesses."

"Furniture making?"

"Yes, and a quilt shop, a bakery, that sort of thing. And then Joshua King's family has King's Cuts and Meats. They do really well during hunting season and it carries them through the winter."

"Sounds like a good place for a man with a trade."

"We do need a blacksmith." Cora smiled, and a moment too late realized how forward that sounded.

But before she could dig herself any deeper, Dean shook his head. "I'm afraid I've decided to settle here. But when Simon Yoder learns his trade, then maybe—"

"Then maybe what?" Simon, who had clearly been talking with someone and hadn't even begun his meal, slid in across from Cora and dug into his heaped-up plate with gusto.

"Once you've mastered the blacksmith's trade, maybe you might head out to Colorado," Dean said. "Cora says that a smith could fill a useful place there."

"She's right," Simon said. "There is no smith in Amity. How long will it take to learn, Dean, to your mind?"

"To master the trade? Seven or eight years."

Simon's fork stopped in midair, and a noodle unwound itself and plopped to his plate.

"That's just to master the basics," Dean went on. "But I'm talking about heavy work—chisels, axe heads, plow blades. Ice tongs and hay hooks. The smaller things you were talking about with Kelvin, well, I don't have any experience there."

"Would finer work take more experience or less?" Cora asked while Simon fell silent. Perhaps he was taking in the magnitude of what he'd signed on for. He couldn't be too fussy about his trade, though. Most young men got started as apprentices when they left school at fourteen. Simon was seven years older than that, and had attempted two trades that she knew of, yet was no further along.

"It might take less," Dean allowed. "Once you get familiar with how the shop works, and the character of the various metals, you could probably make some small things pretty quickly."

"Like five years?" Simon asked.

"More like five months," Dean said. "Give or take. Some men really have a knack for metal. Kelvin, now. He understands it. Sometimes I think he talks it into doing what he wants it to. You'll just have to see, once you get started."

"I hope I can put in an order for a row of coat hooks," Cora said, to be encouraging. "My youngest brother knocked over the coat tree by the door at home and made an awful mess. Mamm said she'd put hooks on that wall like we have in the school coatroom, and he'd keep it tidy just out of habit."

"Consider the order placed." Simon's eyes crinkled and for a moment, Cora forgot where she was. Forgot the months of unhappiness that lay between them. Instead, she was right back at a singing in Amity hugging to herself the delicious knowledge that Simon would take her home afterward, and he would kiss her, and she would close her eyes and taste his mouth and fall up into the stars where anything was possible.

"Cora?" Dean said. "This cherry slice is yours if you want it. I'm a chocolate chip cookie man myself."

She came back to the real world with a bump.

"*Denki*, Dean." She finished her supper and took the cherry slice.

Got up and helped clear the tables.

Helped dry the dishes with the other girls.

And all the while she made a point of not looking at Simon again. It was far too dangerous, this slipping back in time.

Happiness with him was a mirage, and if she had any sense she'd remember that.

Their hosts signalled to the younger ones to bring back the song books, and the second half of the singing got under way. Once again Joe politely asked Cora to begin as *Vorsinger*, so this time she chose an *Englisch* hymn, "I am His, and He is Mine."

Singing was her safe place. Immersed in the music, in the beauty of the words, she could forget about everything and draw closer to God. And while the Whinburg Township *Youngie* were a little bit shy about lifting their voices in harmonizing parts, it was still beautiful when even the hesitant ones tried to join in and add to the sound. In church, no one would dream of doing anything so *hochmut*, so prideful, drawing attention to themselves by singing other than the unified melody. But here, in the Byler home, some could experiment with alto or tenor and enjoy it, even if sometimes they didn't hit the notes quite right. It didn't matter. What mattered was praising God with their whole being—heart, lungs, diaphragm, lips, tongue.

When the last notes of the final song of the evening died away, the chatter rose to take its place. Cora kept an eye on the Zucker sisters so she wouldn't miss her ride home as she talked with some of the girls who had been helpers at Amanda's wedding.

When she turned away, she was greeted by the sight of both Simon and Dean Yutzy making their way through the crowd, heading in her direction.

Oh no. Oh dear, no. She was not about to make a spectacle of herself, first by being *Vorsinger* and second by being someone from out of town catching the eye of not one but two of the local young men.

Drastic action was called for.

With a murmured excuse, she slipped away behind the knot of girls and followed the sound of laughter to the nearest Zucker sister.

"Amy, will you be leaving soon, do you think?"

"Why?" The girl's long-lashed blue eyes were merry. "Is there someone who would like it if you stayed a little while?"

"No, not at all," Cora said as calmly as she could. "I need to be getting back to my cousin, is all. If you aren't ready to go, I can catch a ride with anyone who lives in Whinburg, if you'll point them out to me."

"Here's the very person," Amy said cheerfully. "We'll be leaving soon, but it looks like he'll be leaving sooner. Dean, Cora is getting anxious about Mollie. Would you be able to give her a ride?"

"Of course," Dean Yutzy said with a smile. "I was just on my way to hitch up."

Cora resisted the urge to close her eyes and admit defeat. Clearly *der Herr* was out to make a point tonight. There was going to be no end of talk and teasing now, and there was absolutely nothing she could do about it.

The last thing she saw as she went out the door was Simon, gazing at her and looking as pained as though someone had just stepped hard on his foot.

7

I hope this is all right," Dean finally said when they were safely out of the Byler lane and heading for Old Bridge Road and the county road into Whinburg. "You're awfully quiet."

"I'm sure there's going to be talk." Cora roused herself from gloomy contemplation of that very thing. "What with me being a visitor and all."

"Talk?" He paused, and then in a rush said, "You mean about you and me? Because I ate supper with you and am driving you home?"

Goodness, could anyone be so unaware of the consequences of their own actions?

"Can you think of anything else?" She tried to smile to turn it into a joke, but the interior of his buggy was dark. It was also so new that she could still smell the glue in the wood-panelled dashboard. He was too old to have the dingle-dangles the boys sometimes hung across the top of the window, and since he was a church member, of course there was no battery-powered radio or speakers. This buggy was as plain and proper as could be. How funny, when its driver was as nice-looking and—frankly—improper as could be and completely clueless about it.

"I don't know what," he confessed. "I've driven one or two girls home, but I don't remember people talking about that."

Cora realized she would have to speak plainly. "It's because I'm a visitor. I have no right to spend time with any Whinburg boy when I'm going home at the end of the month. Any relationship would have to end ... or go on long distance."

"Relationship!" Dean glanced at her, and in the light of the street lamps she could swear it was with alarm. If the situation hadn't been so awkward, she would have giggled.

"Yes," she said gently. "People think you are courting me."

"Holy smokes." For a moment, the reins went slack on his horse's back, and the animal looked over its shoulder as though asking him what he thought he was doing. He recovered himself and took control once more. "Is that what you—I mean, have I given you the wrong impression?"

It was the first really personal question he had asked her.

"I ... it did occur to me that you might be interested," she said carefully. Because it was becoming clearer by the second that she had indeed had the wrong impression. Well, who wouldn't?

"Oh, my." He hunched his shoulders under his coat and looked for all the world like a man trying to disappear. "*Ach, neh.* Cora, I'm so sorry."

"Well, I guess that settles that little misunderstanding," she said. "The rest of the township might take a little longer to come to it, though."

"Do—do you think Mollie—does she think I'm courting you?"

Cora stared at him for one long moment. And in that moment, all the pieces fell into place.

"It's Mollie," she said on a note of realization. "You came back to the township because of *Mollie*. You came tonight to hear news of her."

"*Ja,*" he said on a groan. He brought the horse to a halt at the stop sign at the county road. "What a mess I've made of everything." His horse, clearly observing that there was no oncoming traffic, moved forward, and he gathered his wits enough to turn the animal toward town.

"Does she know you have feelings for her?" Cora asked.

He shook his head. "I have been trying to figure out how to begin a courtship, but other than marching up to her door and asking if I can see her point blank, I don't know how to do it."

"There's nothing wrong with marching up to the door and asking," Cora pointed out. "Being straightforward would prevent this kind of misunderstanding."

"But what if she's heard what people are saying? What if the Zucker sisters have been speculating?"

"What if they have? They've been wrong."

He gave a long sigh. "I'm so bad at this."

"Why should you be?" Cora asked curiously. "You're settled, you have a good trade, you don't frighten away small children and animals when you look at them. Why shouldn't Mollie welcome you if you came over to visit?"

"Because what you said earlier condemned me."

"Oh." What was it Savilla King always said? *The tongue weighs practically nothing, but it's surprising how much effort it takes to hold it.* When was she going to learn that lesson? "Dean, for goodness sake, don't listen to me. I didn't mean you. Of course

Mollie would be glad to see you if you stopped by as an old friend. And then you simply take it from there."

"But how? She can't go out with me for a ride, and I won't see her at church for another two weeks."

Cora thought quickly. "Then do things for her. Practical things and silly things. You want to begin as an old friend and then help her see you want something more."

They were passing through Whinburg now, quiet and closed at this time of night. They'd be home soon.

"Silly things are going to help with that?" He sounded as though he'd already given up hope.

"In January, a bouquet of flowers is silly," she pointed out. "But Mollie loves flowers."

"Oh," he said as though this had never once occurred to him. "So I should do things for her—the practical. And bring a gift now and again—the silly. Do I have that right?"

She smothered a smile. "Exactly right."

He heaved a sigh of relief. "What a good friend you are, Cora."

"I love her," she said simply. "Tell you what. As I think of things she'd like, I'll write them down and give them to you. After all, I see her at nearly every hour of the day and we talk all the time."

"Good idea." He pulled up at the bottom of the walk up to the house. "And the first thing on list number one is to shovel off that walk."

"What—now?"

"Maybe not now," he acknowledged, "since it's dark. But first thing tomorrow. The bakery will be open, and we don't want a customer to slip and fall with their bread, do we?"

"I should say not. And maybe Mollie might be persuaded to walk with me to the end of it when it warms up."

"That's a plan." He turned to her. "*Denki*, Cora, for setting me straight. I've been keeping my feelings inside ever since I came back to Whinburg Township, and then when you said—"

"Forget what I said," she told him hastily.

"But you were right. Why would Mollie take me seriously when I started coming around after her operation and not before?"

"When she understands that you were shy, and didn't know how to begin a courtship, she won't think that at all." She slid the door aside and hopped down. "*Guder nacht*, Dean. Careful on the way home."

"*Guder nacht*. I'll do my best. My head is full and so is my heart right now."

He clucked to his long-suffering horse and the buggy disappeared into the crisp night. Cora let herself into the warm house, then checked that the light under Mollie's bedroom door was out.

What had Dean's family and former church district been like that he was so backward when it came to dating? For her, and she supposed for many girls, it was a process. You started taking notice of boys when you were fourteen or fifteen, but you couldn't do anything about it until you were sixteen and allowed to go to singings and do things with the *Youngie*. Lots of group activities and opportunities to be with boys, to talk to them, to see who would make a good partner in games, in conversation, in love, in life together.

And then you prayed about it. She took off her bucket-shaped Colorado covering, released her hair from its pins, and brushed it out. Maybe that was where she and Simon had gone wrong. She had been so dazzled by him, so anxious for every moment they could spend together, that she had forgotten to look to *der Herr* for his approval. She had taken her own way, done what she wanted, without waiting for Him to speak.

Cora knelt by her bed on the braided rug that Mollie had made.

Lieber Gott, I have been so foolish. Here I was, praying that you would send me the partner you wanted for me, and then assuming Simon was the one without even asking you. Draw me closer to you, keep me in the circle of your love so that I can hear clearly when you speak to me. Help me to be a good friend to Mollie, and if it is your will that she finds happiness with Dean, use me to encourage him to be brave. I pray for Simon, too. I think he is lost. Bring him closer to you, lieber Vater in Himmel, so he can see your will for his life and find his joy in it. Be with your people everywhere, I pray, and bless them in their service to you. Amen.

❧

IT TOOK everything Simon had to greet Dean Yutzy politely on Monday morning. He'd had all weekend and an off Sunday to stew about Friday night, the image of Cora climbing into Dean's buggy frozen in his memory like an *Englisch* photograph. That image persisted as Dean and Kelvin showed him around the smithy, pointing out where the tools were kept, where the metal stock was stored before it was worked, and the safety equipment he'd need to use—gloves, safety glasses, fire extinguisher. Kelvin also took him into the office and ran through the order process, in case he was alone in the shop and someone needed to schedule some work done.

"We do farrier work here, like the sign says," Kelvin explained, "as well as on location. I'm not out so much in the winter, because the field horses aren't working so hard, but there are still plenty of buggy horses needing shoes. So I do that two days a week. If a man needs a horse shod, he'll call and either you or Dean will take down the information. *Gut?*"

Simon nodded. "Does Dean go out as well?"

"*Ja*, he does, and so will you when you learn to make horseshoes and put them on. I hear you're good with horses."

Simon shrugged modestly. "We Amish boys were responsible for the horses on the ranch where I worked. I helped the farrier when he came. He was the kind of man who would teach as he worked, so I learned a bit, too."

"There's learning, and there's doing," Kelvin said, and waved at the phone on the desk. "No personal calls, of course. That phone is strictly for the business."

Simon would never have done so in any case, but he tried to stay humble. "I understand."

"Eat your lunch when you're hungry. Remember, one person needs to be in the smithy when we're not working, to take orders, and two when we are, for safety."

Simon nodded again.

"Now, come with me and man the bellows. We'll begin with our best friend, the fire, and by the end of the week I'll be showing you how to run the drill press."

"It's unmodified? Runs on a generator?"

"*Ja.*" The corners of Kelvin's lips quirked up about an eighth of an inch, which Simon took for a smile of approval. "You're observant. That's *gut*. Less chance of accidents with an observant man."

By the end of his first day at work, Simon's arms ached from working the bellows for both Kelvin and Dean, he had taken a telephone order from a hardware store in Strasburg for a dozen hoof picks, and he could check the oil level, gas up, and operate the big Honda generator. This was a business where you learned by doing. Every time Simon learned one thing, the next thing was right there to learn.

"Don't get ahead of yourself," Kelvin warned him. "It's like the Bible says—a house without a good foundation cannot stand. If you learn the principles now, building on them will come naturally."

Strangely, it was easier working with Kelvin than he had anticipated. With Oran, between his own unwillingness for the work of the buggy maker, and his resistance to Oran's authority and knowledge, every task had been a struggle. He could see now that the only surprise was how Oran had tolerated him for so long.

And in Colorado ...

Simon flinched away from his own stupidity. He had lost the treasure in toying with the dross. In his flirting with the rancher's wife, in enjoying the novelty of his effect on a worldly woman, Cora had turned away from him in sorrow and disgust. And the worst of it was, he had known he was making a mistake even as he'd told her he was moving on. Yet he'd done it anyway.

Why? Simon looked at that experience through the lens of hindsight. The answer finally swam up through layers of hurt and pride: Because he had wanted Cora to come after him. To make him change his mind.

What a fool.

Anyone could see that a woman with any self-respect wouldn't do that. No wonder she would hardly say a word to him. Now his job was to become the man he should have been back then. To become the kind of man she could love again.

Because she had loved him. He had known it, and something inside him had been astonished at that—had needed her to prove it. But Cora didn't need to prove anything to anyone.

It was his job to prove himself to her. And to do that, he would lift and sweat and burn his hand because he forgot the safety gloves ... all for her. He would attain by the sweat of his brow what Dean Yutzy seemed to have accomplished with a few short conversations.

But he could not think about that and concentrate on what Dean was saying about the properties of the metal stock they had on hand, and what each was used for. He had to focus on the means of winning Cora back before he had a hope of gaining his ends.

Dean moved along the racks, touching pieces of metal stock here and there as though they were old friends. "We use a variety of steel around here, depending on the job. The higher the carbon content, the harder the steel is."

"How do you tell?"

Dean grinned. "By the sparks flying from the grinding wheel. If the sparks fly away straight, it means the carbon content is low. That makes it softer, easier to heat, bend, forge, file, and drill."

"What about the other?"

"In high-carbon steel, the sparks shoot straight, too, but then they sparkle out like a dill seed cluster."

Simon pictured the dill plants in his mother's garden and immediately saw what Dean meant.

"But the folks at living history places around here, they like us to use the same steel they had in the old days. They make their iron implements and sell them on the spot."

"What about this?" Simon lifted a piece of metal pipe.

"The larger pipe stock is for gate rails and such. The narrower, shinier stuff is what Kelvin uses to repair *Englisch* machinery and for plumbing."

Simon tapped the pipe on one of its companions to

produce a ringing clang. "How do you cut it to length?"

Dean pointed. "Metal band saw. Also powered by the generator. But it will be a while before you work with the tools that use electricity. You have to start at the beginning as our forefathers did, making things by hand."

"I know," Simon admitted. "But it's nice to have an idea of what can be done."

"*Ja,* I remember. You're the man with the ideas."

"Nothing wrong with that." Simon's instinct was to put his hackles up like one rooster challenging another, but he took a deep breath instead.

"*Neh,* I never said there was. I'm not really an idea man, but someone needs to have them. Otherwise there would be nothing for the rest of us to do."

Simon felt a prickle of surprise at the confession. But why should he be surprised? Humility was important in a person's character, and if you had taken your own measure, why not be honest about it? "Well, as you say, best for me to learn the basics of the craft first, then worry about the ideas, *nix?*"

Dean smiled. "There's an order to everything, from the stars *Gott* put in the sky to the salt I put on my food. My Daadi used to say that."

"We just have to learn the order," Simon agreed. He gave the piece of pipe a flick with a fingernail and quietly, it sang the same note. Then he followed Dean across the shop to take his place at the bellows once more.

By Wednesday, he thought his arms would fall off if he had to pump the bellows one more time. "You have to build your strength," was all Kelvin would say when it was clear Simon was operating in some discomfort. It was a relief that afternoon when his employer decided they should start the new year with taking inventory, since business was a little slow.

When the telephone rang, Simon was closest, and Kelvin nodded at him to get it.

"Whinburg Smith and Farrier," he said in English.

"Simon? *Ischt du?*"

His breath caught in his chest at the sound of Cora's voice. "*Ja, ischt mir.* What can I do for you, Cora?"

"I'm calling from the Sugar Sisters Bakery upstairs. I wonder if you might pass a message on to Dean? Two messages, actually. The first is that we wonder if he might have time to stop by on the way home from work. One leg of Mollie's walker has got bent somehow, and maybe he knows how to straighten it?"

Simon's heart seemed to take a nose dive. "I could fix that for her."

Cora hesitated. "Well, I know you probably could, but ... we wondered if it would be more convenient for Dean."

So this was what rejection felt like. Not the kind where you'd missed out on paying work, but the personal kind, where a person came right out and said they didn't want to see you. They wanted to see someone else. Had he really made Cora feel this way last summer and then gone on about his own selfish business?

He could barely bring himself to say, "*Ja*, of course. I'll pass that on. What was the second message?"

"Oh, the Zucker sisters were talking about having a bigger display rack for the bread, since it's so popular among the *Englisch* folks here. Amy, the store manager, would like to make an appointment to come and talk the project over with Kelvin."

The appointment book lay open on the desk, with only a few of the blocks filled in for this first week of January. "Would today suit? Say four o'clock?"

"Just a minute." He heard her muffled voice confirming the time, and she came back on. "*Ja*, that would be *gut. Denki*, Simon."

"Cora—"

"'Bye."

And before he could get out another word, she had disconnected, as though she had no interest in hearing anything he had to say.

In the next moment, her voice flared to life in his memory. *Simon, please just tell me what's wrong, what I've done to—*

He had walked away, leaving her with her questions unanswered ... and likely a feeling just like this squeezing her throat. He hadn't even noticed at the time. Just wanted to escape the consequences of his blunt words as quickly as possible.

What a horrible person he had been only six months ago. How had anyone put up with him? What on earth had Cora found in him to love?

"Simon?" Kelvin called. "Who was that on the telephone?"

He gathered up his thoughts, sharp as broken china, and walked out into the shop to relay both messages.

"Amy Zucker at four, hey?" Kelvin glanced at the clock over the shop door. "Best get this stock counted and our supplier orders written up, then, if we only have two hours."

Promptly at four o'clock, the job done and the sun nearly down on its brief winter circuit of the Pennsylvania sky, a knock came on the shop door.

Kelvin showed Amy Zucker in. She carried a pink bakery box.

"I heard you were a chocolate chip cookie man," she said to Dean, a pair of enchanting dimples denting her creamy cheeks, "so I brought you all a box."

Simon looked from one to the other. She'd heard that from

Cora. Cora was talking to her friends about Dean now. A girl would only do that if she was fairly sure a man was interested.

"That's very kind of you, Amy," Kelvin said gruffly. "You didn't have to."

"Oh, I know," she said, the dimples flashing again. "But they'll be awfully good with your coffee tomorrow, won't they?"

No one was about to dispute such an obvious truth. "I'll put your horse in the shed," Simon offered. When he returned, Amy was nodding over a couple of sketches Kelvin had drawn on the back of some packing paper.

"We were thinking of something a little decorative," she said, and made a swirling motion with her hands. "We've seen that twisted metal—can we have the fronts made of that? And then the shelving should be thin wood planks, with a glossy finish."

Kelvin added a whorl and flourish to the shelf fronts, which acted as stops, and sketched in some boards, tilted down in the way Simon had seen in the *Englisch* grocery stores, to show the bread to advantage. "Like this?"

She clapped with delight. "*Ja*, just like that. But not the feet—the bottom should be solid. We don't want it going over if a little boy decides to climb up to get a hot-cross bun."

"Probably best not to be a free-standing unit, then, but bolted to a wall here and here." Kelvin indicated the bolt points. "We'll make the uprights plain square rods, to make that possible."

"Whatever you think is best," Amy said. "And we'll be sure to tell everyone who made it."

"We appreciate that, Amy," Kelvin told her. "Next Friday all right for delivery?"

"So soon?" Her eyes widened.

"New Year's tends to be slow in many trades," Dean

offered. "We're glad for the work."

"And young Simon here may get his chance to learn to twist iron," Kelvin said. "This is just the kind of project he would like."

Kelvin was as good as his word. Before he went home that evening, Simon had learned how to estimate the metal stock and finishing parts they would need, how much wood Dean should purchase at the lumber yard, and got up close and personal with the metal he would be working with tomorrow.

"This is a *gut* job for you," Kelvin told him as they put on their coats. "It's also going to be challenging, knowing that the project will be seen by the public."

Simon nodded, swallowing a tingle of doubt in his ability to do this so soon. "We want to do our best for the bakery, because our work is part of theirs now."

"Just like we are in church together," Dean said, winding a grey muffler around his neck in loops.

"Are you going over to Mollie Graber's?" The words came out of Simon's mouth before he could stop them.

Dean looked a little surprised. "*Ja*, I was thinking of having a look at her walker now. Why?"

"*Ach*, no reason. *Guder owed*." Mollie and Cora would probably invite Dean to dinner as a thank-you for the small repair to the walker. And after dinner, Mollie would discreetly disappear and …

Simon stalked across the yard to harness Comet. "Maybe I should drive over to the house, too," he told the horse as he fastened his buckles. Always a good listener, Comet flicked an ear in his direction. "To let Zucker girls know the estimate, maybe." But no, that would be stepping on Kelvin's toes.

As he backed the horse out of the shed, he wondered what kind of man he'd become, with no one to talk to but a horse.

❧ 8 ❧

Since returning from California at Thanksgiving, Hannah Riehl had fallen into the habit of walking up the lane every afternoon to collect the mail. She'd had only the post-card and one letter from Ben Troyer, but hope sprang eternal and every day there was the possibility of another.

It sounded like he was pretty busy, though, being man-of-all-work for a rich artist whose life didn't seem to include much of anything.

Hannah had thought she'd worked hard in her previous life as an *Englisch* girl, but now she knew the real definition of it. There wasn't so much of it in the winter, now that the garden was dormant and the grass didn't need to be mowed, but in an Amish household, cleaning and laundry and cooking never went away.

And strangely, she kind of liked it. She felt useful for the first time in her life, with her own chores and her own expectations for herself. Time wasn't something to be endured while you waited for some version of a future to happen. As an

Amish girl, there was simply never enough of it while you were busy living your present.

"Going to get the mail?" Samuel came in with an armload of wood and dumped it in the woodbox next to the living-room stove.

"*Ja,*" she said. "*Komm mit?*"

He nodded and waited for her while she put on her coat and boots. He had swept the night's skiff of snow off the front steps this morning, and off the walk, too, and so far no more had come down to spoil his handiwork.

"The whole family knows why you do this," Sam observed as he paced beside her up the lane, each of them walking in a wheel rut.

"I don't mind them knowing. They all know Ben and I were in a *sinful relationship.*" Her tone made its own finger quotes around the words.

"I think Mamm's a bit worried you want to start it up again. That you'll head off and be *Englisch* and she'll never see you for the rest of her days."

"I think Mamm's a bit worried you will, too." She glanced at her brother, who had been changing so gradually she'd hardly noticed. But she noticed now. "Scratch that. You're growing out your hair. And I've seen you making moony eyes in church at the youngest of those girls at the bakery. The curvy one with the big brown eyes—what's her name?"

"Dora. And don't you tell anyone. Especially her."

Hannah mimed zipping her lips closed. "Are you planning to join church, Sam? Because the rumor among us womenfolks is that she might be starting baptism classes in the spring."

"Making friends, are you?" Which wasn't an answer, and he knew it.

"Friends not as good as Amanda, or Cora, but yes, one or

two. Ben's little sister, for one—Sallie. And our sister Barbie is as good and loyal a friend as anyone could ask for. I love that girl." She was silent a moment, their feet crunching in the snow. "I would have had a buddy bunch, wouldn't I, if it hadn't happened?"

It. Being kidnapped by a pair of mentally ill people, both now facing jail time—years and years of living under another name, living someone else's life—now reduced to *it*.

"*Ja*, you would have. Sallie would have been one of them. *Is* one of them."

"But she's already joined church."

"Still your friend."

"Like you're friends with ... who, exactly?"

"Ouch, *Schweschder*."

They had reached the mailbox. Hannah riffled through a bunch of junk mail and found the January issue of *The Budget*. Here was a big fat packet that had to be Mamm's circle letter, come back to her again rich with news and recipes and quilt patterns from *her* buddy bunch, still in touch after all these years. And at the bottom, a thin envelope with Ben's scratchy handwriting and the same return address.

Her brother, of course, noticed her smiling all over her face. "Care to share?"

"Maybe. Some of it."

"I don't want the mushy parts." He made a face. "Here, give me the rest of that."

She handed everything else to him and opened Ben's letter.

Dear Hannah,

Thanks for your letter and all the news. It's hard to imagine my sister Sallie dating—she was always up to her ears in quilt fabric and drawing designs on the backs of envelopes. But I guess we all change. I can't think which Zook twin it is she's interested in. Aren't there two sets of them? Twins run in that family. Funny how things like that fade when we're not around them. Dad knows every single person in the district. I guess he has to, being the bishop.

It's busy around here. In the past week I've managed to finish clearing the wilderness my landlord calls a backyard. His name is Devon, by the way. Devon Perch, like the fish. Look him up on the Internet sometime—he has quite a story, which he told me over margaritas one night. Anyway, now that the brush is cleared, I can see where a massive vegetable garden must have been. He says the women in the religious commune used to grow roses, too, but if they did, I can't find them. Maybe in the spring. Or maybe I dug them up by accident.

In other news, he sold a painting, so he paid me my month's wages in one big lump, plus extra because of the margaritas. I took it down to the bank and opened my own account. Yay me. Halfway to a radiator and new tires.

Sounds like you had fun at Amanda's wedding. The Amish definition of fun, that is. It all seems like a dream to me now. I really want to see you, especially—

"I'm deleting the next part," Hannah said to Sam.

"Denki," he replied, looking relieved.

Devon hired a cook, of all things. It's not like he can't cook, he just doesn't want to. So it's either order in from every restaurant in Santa Cruz that will deliver, risk my burning the house down, or hire someone. I guess when you're rich you can do what you want. Anyhow, her name is Caledonia, Callie for short. She says her dad named her after some woman in an old rock and roll song. But she can cook, so I guess that's the main thing. Her folks are from Jamaica via Toronto and she has a red seal, which I guess means she can cook in any restaurant she wants. Devon must pay really well.

Guess I'll let this do for now. Not a lot of news in land-clearing, except for the scorpion. Luckily I had boots on and he got the worst end of the deal. Devon would have wandered out here in huarache sandals and got stung. There was a black widow spider in the closet in the Airstream, but I made short work of him, too. Guess I'll have to find the time for a serious Amish hausfraa kind of cleaning in there.

Hope you're well. Tell me what you think of full-time Amish life. I want to know, since we're kind of opposites in that way. Say hi to Sallie, and to Sam. He might write if he wants.

Miss you,

Ben

Hannah folded the letter back into its envelope and put it in her apron pocket to reread later.

"It's weird," Samuel said as they began the walk back down the lane.

"What is? Besides the weirdness that is Ben's life now?"

"Just that," her brother said. "He's pretty much living the life he would have had at home, ain't he? Hard outdoor work all day, and a woman in the kitchen making dinner for the family at night."

"You forgot the father figure. The eccentric artist seems to be paying him some kind of wage, which his own father probably wouldn't do."

"Well, *ja*, but the parts Ben hated the most—the way the men work outside and the women work inside, and you get no real choice about your trade because the Amish only do certain things—that's the weird part."

"Seriously?" Hannah glanced at her brother, in his plain wool sack coat and grey cap Mamm had knitted for him, his cheeks reddened with the cold. "That was what bugged him? Not the religious part?"

"I'm not explaining this very well," Samuel confessed. "But it was more the lack of choice. Ben's an independent guy. He chose to bushwhack that artist's garden. But he wouldn't have had a choice about helping Bishop Troyer on the farm. It would have been expected."

"Sure he would. Simon Yoder doesn't work his grandpa's farm, he chose to be a blacksmith."

"Right, but his uncle is already in partnership with Isaac Yoder, and he'll take it over when the time comes. When you're the bishop's son, and the bishop has a nice farm worth a lot of money, and you're the eldest boy ..."

Hannah began to see. "Poor Bishop Troyer. Who's going to get the farm if Ben doesn't come back and join church?"

Samuel shrugged, watching the narrow track in front of him. "Maybe Sallie will marry a man who likes to farm. Or one of the younger boys will take it over. But it wouldn't be what the family was counting on."

"Maybe that was what got to me in the end, too," she mused aloud. "That I couldn't really count on him. He'd say, oh, you can get a job as a barista anywhere. Not, how about I sign on with that construction crew and make us a few bucks so we can eat."

"He's a hard worker, though," Samuel said. "At the RV factory no one could beat him for speed and accuracy on the construction line."

"Oh, I don't doubt it. But he has to choose it, is the thing. And I guess when we were together, he hadn't chosen what he was going to do. And he has the nerve to say that *I* was impatient." A bubble of annoyance rose in her and burst into words. "I was sleeping in the back of his car and dumpster diving behind the fast food place and *I* was impatient? What happened to the romance of going to California and enjoying the sunshine and surfing all day? It's not what it's cracked up to be, that's for sure."

"Sounds like he's settled now, though."

"Until Mr. Famous Artist decides over the last margarita that he's selling up and going to New York or something. Then Ben is right back where he started."

"With a new radiator and some tires."

"Hopefully."

They went up the steps and Samuel handed her the bundle of mail. "May as well load up some more, since I'm going in."

And there was the difference between Ben and her brother, who had been his best friend. Samuel saw what needed to be done, and just did it. Ben made a big production out of freedom, but when it came down to it, what was he doing with the wonderful luxury of his choices?

Maybe she should ask him in her next letter.

Hannah found her mother and Barbie in the kitchen, frying up thick slices of *Sachwachst* and onions for lunch. "Mamm, your circle letter's come back." She pulled the thick packet out of her pile and laid it at her mother's place at the kitchen table. She tossed the junk mail in the stove, where it flared up and didn't accomplish anything as far as heating the house, then went to the breadbox. As she sliced bread, she said, "I got a letter from Ben."

"How is he?" Mamm always got a crinkle between her eyebrows at the mention of his name. Hannah knew that with every letter, her mother expected Hannah to leave. So far Hannah had managed to smooth that wrinkle, but one of these days she was going to have to make a choice for herself. Exercise her own freedom.

"He's okay. Still at that artist's place, clearing brush. The guy hired a cook, so at least he'll get regular meals."

"That's it?" Barbie asked. She was seventeen now, her little sister, and making the boys look twice. Hannah sometimes marveled at the upwelling of love for her siblings, but in particular this one. After all, Ashley—no, Leah—had gone through the kidnapping and alternative life with her. Yet her feelings for Ash were a combination of love and confusion and incomprehension. She knew Barbie and Mamm and Dat loved her the way she knew the sun came up every morning. And yet, since she and Leah had discovered who they really were, she had no idea how Leah felt about her now. It was like trying to look through the ice in a lake. You knew the water was under there somewhere, but you couldn't see it.

"Pretty much," she replied to her sister. Then she grinned. "He stepped on a scorpion and killed a black widow spider in his closet. Those were today's headlines."

Barbie's face crinkled up in disgust. "Yuck. I'm glad we don't live there."

"Me too." Hannah slipped an arm around her waist and gave her a squeeze. "It's an acquired taste, that's for sure." So were leftover hamburgers in the Dumpster. But she'd never in a thousand years tell her family about that. It would upset Mamm, and Hannah couldn't bear to hurt the woman who had suffered for so many years not knowing where her children were. Not until she and Ash had driven into the yard in an *Englisch* car.

Dat came in just then, and Katie and the twins, and everyone sat down to lunch. After the silent grace Hannah had become used to, she dug into her *Sachwachst* and said, "Mamm, who would my buddy bunch have been if I'd never been—you know."

Mamm glanced at her husband, the way she did every time Hannah mentioned *it*. "Well, let's see. Sallie Troyer, whom you've already struck up a friendship with."

"Who else is twentyish?" Barbie mused. She named a couple of the girls who sat with them on the unmarried women's benches at church.

Hannah nodded. Those girls were tight. It would take some doing to break into their circle, but with Sallie's help it could be done.

"Do you always have to be the same age?" Katie wanted to know. "What if I was best friends with Lizzie Mast? She's younger than me."

"A young person's buddies don't have to be the same age," Mamm said. "Usually you're in the same grade at school, and you get to be friends as you come up through the grades. But you can find friends anywhere—in sewing circle, at a wedding, on a trip."

Barbie eyed her, putting away her helping of luscious fried onions before one of the twins reached over to steal them. "Are you looking to make solid friendships, Hannah?"

Here was a make-or-break moment. Friendship implied a desire to stay, to put down roots. "*Ja*, maybe. Sallie has invited me to her sewing circle on Tuesday. I'm not the quilter she is, but I'm up to seven stitches per inch. That's progress."

Barbie grinned. "Considering you didn't know how to sew when you got here, I'd say so."

"It warms my heart to hear you say these things, Hannah," Dat said gruffly. He knew better than to press her, but it was clear he meant every word.

"And mine," Mamm said. "With every choice, we make a life, don't we?"

Hannah nodded. "I like that I have a choice now. When I

was ... taken ... I didn't have one. Not for years after that. I think the first real choice I ever made as a grown-up was to come back here."

"And we thank the *gut Gott* every day that you did," Dat said. "Leah is in our prayers without ceasing. We can only hope she makes the same choice."

Not much hope of that, since she'd begun university and had an *Englisch* boyfriend—both choices that were hard to undo. But you never knew. Hannah had made the choice to go to California with Ben, knowing it would mean a physical relationship with him, an emotional commitment. And she'd managed to undo that, though she'd wondered on the train back how she'd survive the pain of leaving her first love. She hadn't entirely survived it even yet, but the stab in her heart at seeing his handwriting somehow had become more anticipation than loss. Strange. It had only been three months. You'd think pain like that would take more time to heal.

"Barbie, will you come with me to Sallie's thimble party?" she asked her sister. "I'm still not a hundred percent about driving the buggy by myself."

"You do fine," her sister assured her. "And I'd love to go. Millie Troyer is in my buddy bunch, so I'll get to see her."

And so the threads that bound her to her family reached out and bound her to the folks in the church. Every choice was a thread. Every thread was a relationship. And somehow, Hannah thought, it all made up a design. Maybe she couldn't see it yet, but it wouldn't be so bad to be a part of it. To love and be loved. To belong. To have work to do whose results she could see.

And to never, ever eat at a fast food restaurant again.

9

Mollie answered the door, using her cane and moving slowly, since Cora was in the kitchen of the little basement suite making dinner. "Dean," she said pleasantly, and let him in. "We didn't expect you to come today. Any day before church next week would have been fine."

"*Guder owed*, Dean," Cora called. "Will you stay for supper?"

Mollie might have made a sound, but as she was making her slow way back to the sofa, Cora couldn't be sure.

"I—well—only if you have enough. I mean, if I wouldn't impose," he stammered.

Wooden spoon in hand, Cora stepped back so she could see him from where she stood at the gas stove. "We have plenty, and anyone who comes to help could never impose."

"Well then, I'd be happy to. I'll just put my horse in your barn." When he came back ten minutes later, he took off his hat and coat and hung them on the coat tree that held their things. "I'd best look at the walker now, then, and earn my keep."

He pulled a couple of tools from his coat pocket and while Cora tasted her beef stew and saw that it was good, she heard clinks and scrapes coming from the living room. No conversation other than the most polite small talk. Poor Dean might have been an *Englisch* plumber for all the warmth and interest he got.

But she had to stay out of Mollie's business. If her cousin got even one whiff of the possibility that Cora might be matchmaking ... well, Cora wasn't sure what she would do, but she wasn't about to risk it. She was no matchmaker anyway. She couldn't even manage a romance for herself, let alone anyone else.

Since Mollie was avoiding potatoes, she had made wild rice, which she fluffed up and turned into a pretty blue serving bowl made by *Englisch* Henry, if the mark on the bottom was any indication. Simon's stepfather.

But she mustn't think about Simon.

While a pat of butter melted on top of the rice, she cut several slices of the day-old bread they got at half price from upstairs. When everything was on the table, and she'd set a place for Dean, she said, "Dinner is ready."

"And this is done." Dean rose to his feet and set the walker next to Mollie. It looked as good as new.

"I don't need it just to walk to the table," she said. "If you want to wash those hands, the bathroom is down the hall."

Oh dear.

While Dean was in the bathroom, Cora made Mollie comfortable in her usual chair. "What is wrong?" she whispered.

"Nothing." Mollie adjusted her knife next to her plate. "Why do you ask?"

But Dean came out just then and Cora was saved from having to reply.

After saying grace, she handed their guest the rice and then the stew. A heaping helping of coleslaw, the bread, and Mollie's crunchy carrot pickles rounded out the meal.

"*Ach*, this is gut," Dean said. "Did you both do the cooking?"

"*Ja,*" Cora said. "This is a joint effort."

"Making rice and shredding cabbage isn't exactly cooking," Mollie pointed out.

"But without the preparation, there would be no end product," Dean said with a smile.

Mollie tilted her head in acknowledgement and savored a forkful of stew. "Still, I'd like to know what you put in here, Cora. Mine never tastes like this."

"Yours is probably better," Cora said. "Mamm always cuts in a hot chile. Joshua King's sisters grow them because they have a nice south-facing slope and they do well in the soil. Then they make salsa out of them and sell it in the market in Amity. Anyway, that little tingle you taste is the chile. I didn't put in the whole thing in case you didn't like it."

"I like it," Dean said. "If it's the will of God that I marry, maybe you might share the recipe with that future person."

Oh dear. Now it sounded as though he was still waiting, instead of acting on his conviction that God had put Mollie into his heart. As for Mollie, she looked down at her meal as intently as if the will of God might be found in the gravy.

Was Mollie angry that Cora had invited Dean without asking her first? Surely not. She was the most hospitable person in the world, and after all, Dean was doing her a favor. It was natural to want to thank him.

Or was it something more personal? Had Cora been more

right than she knew, and Mollie resented him for paying her attention now when he hadn't before?

Oh, how she hoped not. They were old friends. Surely she knew him better than that.

Maybe that was the key, Cora thought suddenly. She'd advised Dean to come as an old friend at first, hadn't she? But maybe he was so nervous he'd forgotten.

She'd told herself to stay out of it, but if someone didn't say something, he'd go away discouraged and some other girl would swoop in to take advantage of his vulnerable heart.

"Mollie, you and Dean were scholars together here in Whinburg, weren't you?"

"*Ja,*" Mollie said, the word falling with a plop into her stew.

Dean seized the conversational rope eagerly. "We were both in the third grade, I think, when my father brought the family here. You sat with a girl called Anna, if I remember."

"Anna Esch," Mollie said. "She'll be Anna Wengerd soon."

"She is going to marry a man from out our way," Cora explained to Dean. "Neil Wengerd is foreman at the buffalo ranch in our valley."

Dean's eyes widened. "There are ranches for buffalo?"

"Apparently," Mollie said.

Cora added smoothly, "This one is used a lot by movie people when they make westerns. And since buffalo are hard to come by outside of Yellowstone or a national preserve, they use the ranch. The people who own it are conservationists. The animals aren't grown to make steaks and hamburgers out of."

"Have you ever had a buffalo steak?" Mollie asked, showing the first evidence of interest.

"*Neh*, I've never had the opportunity," Cora admitted. "And

I'm not sure I'd want to, knowing that a rare creature had to be killed in order to satisfy my appetite."

"Will your friend Anna be moving to Colorado?" Dean asked Mollie.

"I don't know," she said in a more normal tone. "I don't think they've decided. Her sister is settled here, and her father leases the farm to the Bontragers. There won't be anyone to keep house for him unless he goes with them or they stay here."

"Except the sister," Dean pointed out.

"She has a big family and a farm to help run," Mollie said. "But they do have a *Daadi Haus*. I suppose we'll have to wait and see."

"Has she asked you to be *Neuwesitzer*?" Cora asked curiously. "You're quite close, aren't you?"

Mollie's stony face softened into a smile for the first time. "*Ja*, she has. I'm hoping I'll be able to walk into church with her all on my own. She says I'm to use the cane or the walker if I need to, but it's *gut* to have a goal to work toward. And that's mine."

"As long as they don't have the wedding in the next three weeks, you should be able to do it," Dean said. "Just watch out for next week."

"Cora told me about your *Daadi* and his accident," Mollie said.

Cora dared to feel relief that she'd directed a whole sentence at him.

"I was out of school a lot during those weeks, but there was no one else to keep him company in the *Daadi Haus*," Dean said. "I was grateful for a certain little girl who would share the lessons with me so I wouldn't fall too far behind."

"The teacher sent me over with them," Mollie reminded

him. "Don't make me out to be more generous than I was. Mostly I just wanted to play in those days."

"Didn't we all. And then you grew up to be so lively and interested in doing all kinds of things," Dean said. "Remember the fruit stand? All the *Kinner* along our road would pick a basket of wild blackberries and you and Anna would sell them and split the money among us."

Mollie nodded. "I never could understand why Grannie Yoder never paid attention to her stand. She just took her produce down there and walked away and left it."

"Trusting the honor system?" Cora suggested.

"She was such a humble lady she probably felt a customer honored her by choosing her produce," Dean said, a faraway look in his eyes. "The money in the box was probably just gravy to her. I must say that we kids always put a quarter in there for her. Rent for the space to sell our wild berries, I suppose."

"Those berries tasted so good," Mollie said. "I probably ate more than I sold."

"Me too," Dean confessed with a smile. "You cried like you were heartbroken one time, when the crows got into your basket and made such a mess."

"And you gave me the only quarter you'd earned that day," Mollie said. "I don't think I ever thanked you for it. I just ran home and gave it to Mamm and never told her about the crows— or that I'd left the mess." She looked up at him, and Cora dared to breathe easier. "Thank you, from the *Schisser* that I was."

"You've already thanked me for any small thing I might have done." He smiled into her eyes, and Cora realized that for him, there were only two people at the table. "By inviting me into your home, and to your table."

Mollie's face closed. "Oh, that was Cora." She struggled to her feet, leaning heavily on the table. "Cora, will you be all right cleaning up? I need to take one of those pain pills the doctor gave me, and I'll probably just go to bed."

"*Ja*, of course. Let me help—"

"It's all right. I can manage this much." She walked down the short hall to the bathroom, back straight, steps careful, hands braced on the walls on either side.

When the bathroom door closed, Cora glanced at Dean. His face was still, stricken. He got up as though he didn't quite know where he was. "Did I say something wrong?"

"*Neh*, not at all." She hoped. "It's the pain. Sometimes it makes her short with people."

"*Ach*, poor girl." He gathered his emotions in with a visible effort. "May I help you with the dishes?"

"It's getting late and your horse will be wanting her own barn. I can have these done in ten minutes." Besides, if Mollie heard them out here in the kitchen, talking and laughing, that would do Dean no favors.

"Thank you for supper," he said as he put on his coat. "Both of you. My aunt is a good cook, and I can cook without poisoning myself, but still, that was the best meal I've had in a long time."

"Then I hope you come again." She lowered her voice. "And when you do, bring flowers."

"Believe me, I won't forget."

She closed the door behind him thoughtfully. All in all, this first visit had gone not too badly. She wasn't sure what had turned Mollie's smile upside down, but at least it was a beginning.

A practical gift—the walker. A reminder of their old friendship. Surely a silly thing like flowers in January would open the gate to something more?

*

Cora had to pass Mollie's door on the way to her own room. No light showed under it, but Cora's attuned ear caught a soft sound. A sound any woman would recognize, even if she wasn't a mother.

Cora opened the door just a crack. "Mollie? Are you all right?"

The blankets rustled. "Fine," her cousin croaked.

Obviously she was not fine. Cora slipped into the room, found the foot of the bed by feel, and sat on the end. She did not light the lamp. Sometimes confidences were best exchanged in the dark, the way they had when Mollie was a young bride and Cora came to visit.

"Cora, I love you, but please go away."

"Tell me what's wrong," she said gently.

"You wouldn't understand."

"I might."

The blankets rustled again. "How could you?" Her voice cracked. "You have everything. How could you possibly understand someone who has nothing?"

For a moment Cora was nonplussed. What on earth? "You may be a widow and I've never been married, but both of us are blessed with families who love us and a community where we fit in."

"Do we? You might have those things, but I don't. And now the one thing I thought God was going to give me is snatched away and ..." She choked, and when she next spoke,

Cora could hear by the tone that she had turned her face to the wall. "Just please go away."

Cora wasn't sure how to respond to someone who believed she didn't fit into her own church or family. But there was one problem she thought she could shine some light on.

"Are you talking about Dean Yutzy?"

A high keening of distress was her reply.

"Mollie, truly, you don't have to worry."

"That's very easy to say." Her cousin's voice was thick with emotion and a nose stuffed up from crying. "You're pretty, and talented, and people are talking about the two of you in my hearing. Do you know how painful that is? Worse, he's never come to call before and yet the minute you arrive, he's on the doorstep."

It was time to light the lamp.

Cora did it by feel, and Mollie squinted at her in the flare of the yellow flame. From the top drawer of the dresser, she fetched a neatly folded handkerchief, and waited while Mollie blew her nose.

"First of all," she said, "I've been here for a week, not a minute. And second of all, never listen to 'people.' Dean has been talking to me, that's true. He drove me home from the singing on Friday. Also true. Do you want to know what we talked about?"

"*Neh.*" Mollie wouldn't look at her.

"We talked about you, *Liewi.*"

Mollie's brown eyes locked on hers. "Why?"

"Because Dean Yutzy is the most hopeless man in the world when it comes to courting. He wanted to talk to somebody about you, to find out your feelings and how you were managing. Just to talk about you to someone who knew you well. Namely me."

Silence. The silence of complete disbelief.

"I called him this afternoon to ask him to come over and fix the leg on your walker. I asked him to stay for supper, *ja*, sure. But for your benefit, not mine. And he's going to call again. Not to see me, but to see you."

Mollie's mouth was opening and closing, but no sound came out.

"He wants to court you, *Liewi*. But he's so shy and awkward he doesn't know how to begin. He needed a boost, and I happened to be in the right place at the right time."

"He isn't awkward," Mollie said in a small voice. "He's kind, and funny, and considerate. At least, he was when we were children."

"Our Mammi would say that the ways of a child become the habits of a man, wouldn't she? I don't think Dean has changed in his essentials. And one of those is the way he feels about you. I think he's cared all this time, even when you were married."

Mollie's eyes filled with tears, and she hunted for a dry section of the handkerchief. "You're sure?" she said. "You're not just telling me a story to make me feel better?"

"I'm not much of a storyteller," Cora said dryly. "I'm sorry that people have the wrong end of the stick, but like any puppy, they'll lose interest and drop it, probably sooner than later."

Mollie scrunched the handkerchief in one hand. "I was so rude to him. I'm so ashamed."

"I wondered what was wrong."

"I thought he was calling on you and I just couldn't bear it."

"But you seemed to warm up later on. I was glad to see that."

"It's hard not to be warm, with him," Mollie said softly. "I just wish ..." Her gaze fell to her knees, elevated slightly on a second pillow.

"You'll be able to walk without help in a couple of weeks," Cora said, "and remember what the doctor said. In another six weeks you'll be fully mobile."

"But watch out for week three," she said, a smile curving her lips for the first time.

"If gambling wasn't a sin, I would bet that a certain person will be hovering around here finding things to fix during week three so he can make sure you don't overdo and set yourself back."

The smile widened at the suggestion, and a quiet happiness filled Cora's heart at the sight of it.

"Do you think the girls would mind if we broke a couple of things he could fix?" Mollie asked, mischief filling her eyes.

Cora had to laugh. "This is an old house. I think there are enough things to repair that he won't have any trouble finding reasons to keep an eye on you. Besides, they've ordered a new display rack for the bakery. Maybe he'll even be the one to install it."

Mollie gazed at her. "I'm sorry I was horrible to you. You're such a *gut freind*, I don't know how I could have thought those things."

"You don't really think your family and church don't care about you, do you?"

"Neh," Mollie confessed. "The church has been good about paying the medical expenses, and the Zuckers have gone out of their way to make sure I'm all right. You and your branch of the family are all I've got, though, since Mamm and Dat passed, and my brothers moved to Maryland."

"Why didn't you go with them? I've always wondered."

Mollie lifted her chin. "Because I like it here. Up until recently I worked at the library, and the head librarian said I was welcome back as soon as I was up and around again. I can look after myself ... this is just my season to need a little help."

"And that's what we're here for." Cora took her hand and gave it a squeeze. "I'll say good night. And when I say sleep well, I mean it."

Mollie squeezed back. "I've cared about him a long time, too, you know. But when he moved away and never came back, I got married. My parents expected it, and Jonah was the foreman on the farm. And then when my little Jeremy came along, I stopped thinking about Dean."

"But he never stopped thinking about you," Cora said softly.

"It's a miracle," Mollie whispered. "A gift I never expected."

"And now?"

"I may have more to dream about than I've ever had before."

❧ 10 ❧

Dear Ben,

Thanks for your letter. I read it out loud (well, most of it) to Sam when we got the mail. He's not much of a writer, he says, but he's glad you seem well and that at least you've got lots of experience looking after big vegetable gardens. I guess that was your job—turning over the garden in the spring and helping your mom plant?

Sam also said it seemed funny to him that you had essentially the same life out there that you did here. But with my weird life, I can see both how he would think that and how what you do now isn't the same at all. So don't be mad at him for thinking that.

You wanted to know what I was thinking. Should I stay or should I go, to quote the Kinks. Samuel and I talked a little bit about it. The truth is, I like having a place to belong. I like that I chose to come back, and that I know down deep that Rebecca and Jonathan and Barbie and the smaller ones love me for me. They'd like it if I joined church, of course, but even Jonathan can see that it's going to take a while for this half-Amish girl to learn Deitsch again, and get her head around the Ordnung. Oddly, a lot of the language is coming back, I guess from hearing it all day long. The fam speaks to me in

Deitsch, and if I don't get it, they repeat it in English. I dreamed in it the other night. They say you've nearly learned a language when that happens. It certainly never did when I faked my way through Spanish in high school.

Funny that here, I'm overeducated. Sometimes I think of all the things expected of an Amish woman and get overwhelmed. I mean, I love being here and living day to day. But if I joined church, I know I'd be expected to get married and have a big family. I don't know— can a person stay single and still make her way? Make a living of some kind? Maybe I should open a coffee shop, ha ha. I could call it *A Cup of Kindness.*

I've just never been the sort who oohed over babies and wanted to hold them. Maybe it's because of what happened. Maybe it's genetic. Nature or nurture. Who knows? Barbie got that gene, and probably Katie did too. They love carrying babies around after church and helping them walk and stuff.

Anyhow, all this to say I'm leaning toward this life because of the people in it that I love. Where does that leave us? I'm not sure. Maybe part of me is thinking that you'll get tired of logging and black widows in the closet and come home. Another part thinks, well, if he did and he still doesn't want to be Amish, where does that leave me if I do? I suppose we all have to make up our own minds, but it's hard when other people are affected by our decisions.

This isn't much of an answer to your question, but at least you know I'm thinking about both sides and trying to weigh them. Samuel is, too, though he doesn't talk about it much.

Take care of yourself. I'm glad you're going to be eating proper meals now.

Miss you,
Hannah

Simon could see within a few minutes of Kelvin's beginning work on the bakery shelving unit that Dean had been right—he did talk the metal into doing what he wanted. He had a series of three-eighths square stock heating in the forge that would become the horizontal pieces that kept the bread from sliding out the front, and section by section, added the twist so that the metal became a spiral while still retaining its ability to do its part within the whole. How many years, he wondered, would it take before he could do that? And not even something big, like this, but Cora's coat hooks, for instance. He hadn't brought those up to Kelvin or Dean yet, but he would. He wanted to give them to her before she went back to Colorado ... or as a way of convincing her not to go at all.

"Now you try," Kelvin said, stepping back when there were four or five twists in the first piece of metal.

Simon blurted, "I'd ruin it."

"If you do, just do it over. Once the next section is glowing red, fix the one end in the vise. Then with these tongs, give it a slow turn and even heat. Feel what it does, and do it again. A full turn makes a twist."

Flexing his gloved fingers, Simon stepped forward. The rod wasn't heavy, but if he so much as sneezed, there would be a kink in its length, not a twist. As instructed, he clamped it in the vise, then picked it up and turned it at the same speed he'd seen Kelvin use.

"Not so fast," came from behind him. "Take your time and feel what it's telling you."

It felt like it wanted to turn, now, before the heat melted right through it. Simon turned it again, slower this time.

"Again."

One more turn. He dared to put the next few inches into the heat. When it glowed red, he gave it a turn. Once, then twice.

"*Gut*. Keep going."

The door to the office slammed and Dean came in from his errand. Simon's attention was distracted for just a second—just long enough for him to loosen his grip on the rod. His tongs slipped—the rod bent—

"*Ach, neh!*" He'd ruined it! Would Kelvin take the cost of the rod out of his pay? He'd completely deserve it if so.

"Here." The smith nudged him out of the way and made the rod look delicate as he took it in his capable hands. "Just get it glowing red and hammer it back into shape."

A few expert strokes and the rod was straight again.

"Metal is more forgiving than we think if it gets bent out of shape. More forgiving than a few people I know." With a smile, he stepped aside and let Simon take it up again.

In less than an hour, he had completed all six front pieces and only had to use the hammer one more time. His body was running with sweat, not from the forge—though that was pretty hot—but from worry that he'd ruin the project. His hands shook from clamping his fingers so hard.

"It gets more natural with time," Kelvin said. "You did well."

Simon could hardly believe the man was being straight with him.

"For now, I want you and Dean to use the cutter together. It's a two-man job to cut these lengths of three-eighths to size for the side pieces."

"Measure twice, cut once," Simon repeated from a previous experience at the buggy shop that had resulted in the cost of a piece of fiberglass coming out of his pay.

"Exactly," Kelvin said with that subtle smile.

Simon fired up the generator for Dean, they both put on their safety glasses, and then Simon paid close attention to each step in the use of the saw. He had no desire to lose a finger or even the tip of a glove to that wicked blade.

The length had been written out on the order form from the measurements Amy Zucker had provided, so while Simon measured (twice), Dean cut. Halfway through they traded places.

"I know Kelvin said you should learn the machinery later," Dean told him, "but it makes sense to learn it as you need it, too. Lucky business is slow and we have time to teach you."

Simon lowered the saw carefully, cutting exactly where the white soapstone mark lay on the stock. "And these will be twisted, too?"

"*Neh*, the uprights have to be square so we can bolt the shelves to them. I'll go to the bakery tomorrow to locate the studs in the wall and confirm the width," Dean went on. "When we get all this cut, I'll use the drill press to make holes in the four brackets I made this morning. Those will hold the uprights to the wall. You can just watch me for that one. It's trickier than the saw."

Simon's attention had got stuck on *I was over last night*. "Did you see Cora and Mollie while you were there?"

"*Ja*, sure. I took a little thank-you present with me. Which I guess was a thank-you for the thank-you." He chuckled.

"Meaning...?"

"Oh, they invited me to dinner after I straightened the leg on Mollie's walker. It wasn't bent that bad—hardly seemed anything worth a helping of Cora's stew. She can cook, that girl. Good as anything I ever tasted, and pecan pie for dessert on top of it."

A wave of emotion rolled over Simon that had a nasty undertow to it. It took him a moment to realize that this wasn't anger—it was jealousy.

Jealousy, the green-eyed monster, the sin that produced a hundred others. He'd never felt it before. It was horrible. He knew he had a reputation in the township for being a flirt. That didn't bother some girls—they wanted someone who was fun and didn't ask much of them. They got serious with other boys, not him.

This was different. Cora was different.

And Dean was staring at him. "You going to give me that next section or not?"

Simon collected himself and measured out the next section, marking it with the soapstone. Dean had just brought the saw down on his mark when he realized he hadn't double-checked his measurement against the order form.

"Wait!"

Too late. The saw blazed through the stock and the result came away in Dean's hand, too short to use.

"I'm sorry, Dean," he said, his shoulders slumping. "I didn't re-check it. It's my fault."

Dean shook his head. "Happens to all of us. Give me those little upright lengths. All three inches, right? We'll just make as many as we can out of this one so it isn't wasted."

"Why didn't I think of that?" Simon groaned. "*Ja*, three inches. Let me mark it."

"When you've miscalculated as many times as I have, you get pretty good at making silk purses out of sows' ears. Don't let it bother you. Usually there's another use you can make out of any mistake."

Simon measured out his marks—checking twice—and Dean began the cuts.

"So," he said casually, "I guess Cora's taken over the cooking, then? That's a pretty nice thank-you, all right."

"Looks like, for now." Dean stacked the three-inch pieces on the bench and waved a hand for the next longer piece. Simon measured it, marked it, and handed it to him. "But Mollie is getting around better and better. Cora does exercises with her every day, and they've started walking circles around the house. Cora measured the distance with her measuring tape, she says. Each circuit is a hundred feet. They aim for three hundred feet every day."

Simon's hands tightened on the metal at the thought of Dean's knowing so many small details of Cora's life. How was she going to take him seriously if Dean was always there?

"Do they have any other things that need done around the place?" he asked in what he hoped was a casual tone. "That house is pretty old. The Zucker girls kept a pair of carpenters pretty busy when they first bought it, but they couldn't afford a complete remodel. It would be too much for anyone except an actual builder."

"You're right there. *Ja*, they put most of their money into the bakery, which is where the living room and dining room were before that house got divided into three sections. The bottom bedroom is the office now, and the kitchen, of course, is the baking part. They've got new gas ovens, three of them. State of the art, they tell me."

"So a handy person could probably help them out."

"I suppose," Dean allowed. And then he waved for the next piece of stock, and the subject dropped.

But as they worked, Simon was already concocting a plan.

At the end of the long but productive day, after he'd washed the oil and soot from his hands and arms at the utility sink, on his way out of the shop Simon again passed the rack of tubing. His mind busy with possibilities of things he could do to help around the Zucker house and bakery, he flicked a tube in passing. Once again it gave that ringing sound. Not as clear as when Cora sang that note, but not bad for a piece of metal tubing. He flicked another one, still thinking. It gave a different tone. Higher. Because it was shorter.

He flicked the two pieces one after the other and to his surprise they harmonized.

Turning, he went into Kelvin's office, where his employer was lining up orders by date for the rest of January. "Kelvin, what did you say we used the tubing for?"

He sat back in his wooden ladderback chair and gazed at Simon. "Gates. Pipes that need to be custom fit. Once in a while fine plumbing, like in RVs that need smaller pipes."

"Have you ever made wind chimes?"

Slowly, Kelvin's brows rose. "You mean those things people hang outside that make such a racket? No. We spend our time on useful things here. Not decorations."

"But if I wanted to make a gift for someone, would you object if I bought the stock and did it on my own time?"

Kelvin thought for a moment. "I suppose not. But you haven't learned to use the bandsaw yet. Or the sander, for the ends of the cut tubes."

"Dean taught me how to use the bandsaw."

Kelvin shook his head. "I never saw a man in such a hurry. But you did well today, and I'll probably let you finish up all the twisted rods tomorrow."

Which seemed to be permission of a sort. "*Denki*, Kelvin."

"Do you know what lengths you want to cut? You have to be precise with those, you know. A quarter inch off and your chime will sound like breaking china."

"I'll have to find out. Otherwise I'll go through the whole

rack trying to learn which lengths produce what sound. I have a certain sound in mind."

His boss eyed him. "You do, do you?"

With a nod, Simon said, "A friend of mine writes songs. I thought maybe the first couple of notes of one of the songs would make a good chime and a nice present."

Kelvin shook his head. "You must've driven Oran Yost crazy. But I don't object to a man using the brain *der Herr* gave him. As long as you don't cost me anything, and you don't cut off any body parts, you go right ahead and build your silly, useless wind chimes. On your own time."

Simon grinned. "Somebody must think they're useful. I see them on people's verandahs, just for pretty."

"Not Amish verandahs."

His mother had one, its tubes made of fired clay, given to her by Henry, but Simon kept his mouth shut. It did give him another idea, though.

He wished Kelvin good night, and went out to harness Comet. When he got home, Caleb was already at the table and Henry was washing up at the sink.

While Sarah took a baked lasagna out of the oven and put it on top of the stove to cool a little, Simon helped her set out the other dishes—what she called a "crunch salad," with broccoli and cauliflower; boiled green beans with bacon and onions; bread; and the beet pickles both he and Caleb loved.

"*Denki*, Simon." Sarah smiled at him as she put the lasagna pan on the table and cut helpings for them.

After their silent grace, the kitchen was filled with the clatter of a hungry family digging into their supper. "How did your day go today?" Caleb asked him, shoveling in lasagna as though he thought there might not be seconds in the huge pan. "Did you set anything on fire?"

"Pretty close." While Sarah looked up, faintly alarmed, with one hand Simon ruffled up his little brother's hair until Caleb batted it away. "I learned to twist square stock, so technically it glowed red hot, it didn't melt or catch on fire. The rods were for the front of a new bread display rack in the Sugar Sisters Bakery."

"Kelvin's not wasting any time with you, is he?" Henry looked impressed. "That doesn't sound like baby steps to me."

"To be fair, the smithy is kind of slow this week, so it's a good time for training," Simon admitted. "If they were busy, they'd probably keep me on bellows duty or sweeping up the shop for the first month. Kelvin is a strict man, but flexible, too. If a job includes something advanced, like using the band-saw, he lets me do it as long as Dean is right there."

Sarah nodded. "If a patient needs a complicated recipe, there's no point in going halfway—I would learn how to do the complicated part in order to give them what they need."

"*Ja*, just so." He helped himself to more beet pickles and turned to Henry. "I got a little idea of something to make in my spare time. Wind chimes, like you made for Mamm, only out of metal."

Henry nodded, his mouth full of lasagna. Everyone loved it when Mamm made it, melting with gooey cheese and a layer of spinach inside, and luscious homemade tomato sauce.

"I wonder how you made the clay tubes sound right, though?"

Henry gave a mighty swallow. "I toyed with learning to play the piano when I was *Englisch*. I learned about intervals—how notes harmonize together depending on how far apart they are. After that it was arithmetic. A certain length of tube produces a certain sound. If you want your intervals to be thirds—" He hummed two notes. "—you cut them according to the length that will produce those notes."

Simon leaned forward. "Do that again."

Henry hummed the two notes. Simon hummed the second one while Henry held the first. "That's what the *Youngie* do in Colorado," Simon said on a note of discovery. "Most of them sing a third apart. But what about this?" He hummed the first phrase of the song Cora had made up.

"Okay, from the first note it goes up a third, a sixth, and a fourth. The third and fourth are right next to each other on the scale, so they're going to clash if your chimes hold the vibration for any length of time." Henry ate a mouthful of beans. "Then it's not a chord anymore—it's discord."

Simon's shoulders slumped. "That's no good, then." He cast back in his memory for another of Cora's songs, his fork motionless over his plate. "What about this?"

He hummed another phrase that the Swarey family had sung together when he'd been there for supper one night.

"That would work," Henry said. "Your beginning note, two thirds, the octave, and back to the second third. Five chimes— four really, since one repeats."

"You could make the repeating one higher," Sarah suggested.

Slowly, Simon nodded. "I could. I can hear it in my head. So how do you know how long to cut each chime to make that note?"

"Out of metal?" Henry shrugged. "You've got me. I used clay and a lot of trial and error."

"You could go to a tourist shop in Strasburg and see how long theirs are," Caleb suggested. "But they're probably closed in the winter."

"Would it be on the Internet?" Simon asked.

"Everything is on the Internet," Henry said with a laugh. "There's probably some craftsman out there with all the fractions and equations for wind chimes all laid out."

"How late is the library open?" Sarah asked. "Until eight, *nix*?"

Simon hadn't been in the library in a few years, but that was about to change. "It's too late now," he said, "but I'll get there, maybe after work Monday. I'm going to find out how to make wind chimes sing Co—these songs."

"I have something that might help," Henry said. He glanced at Simon's mother. "Do you have any objection to Simon having my old mouth organ?"

"Have you kept it all this time?" She looked amused. "You got that when you were on *Rumspringe*, didn't you? Years and years ago."

"Don't make me sound ancient." Henry sounded stern, but Mamm's eyes twinkled.

"No, I don't mind, as long as it stays in the family."

Henry got up. "Be right back."

The sound of someone rummaging in the storage room upstairs made Simon and Caleb tilt their heads up, as though they could see through the ceiling. "A mouth organ?" Caleb wondered out loud. "They still make those?"

In a few minutes, they could hear Henry's footsteps coming down the stairs. "Found it," he announced, and handed over a battered box about the size of a chocolate bar and twice as deep.

He showed Simon how to play it, then how to find the intervals. "It only has one key," he explained. "That means what chord a song is based on and how many sharps and flats it has. But if you're trying to remember melodies while you're cutting tube lengths, it could help."

Simon breathed into the mouth organ and sure enough, out came the first notes of Cora's song. When he looked up, he was grinning, and Henry grinned back.

"It definitely helps."

"Now that you have that settled," Sarah said, moving over to stand beside her husband, "we have a little news for you two."

Henry took her hand and gazed down into her eyes.

And Simon suddenly knew what they were going to say.

"We're going to welcome one more to our family in the spring," Sarah said, her hand going to her belly in a gesture as ancient as humanity itself. How had he not noticed that his mother had put on a little weight?

Because you're too busy with yourself. Always yourself, and not others. The little voice in the back of his mind sounded a lot like his father, with a bit of Mammi mixed in. And the little voice was probably right. He needed to do better, for his family's sake. Who knew how different his own life might have been—how different his relationship with Cora might have been—if he'd paid attention to that little voice sooner?

Caleb whooped and moved in for a hug, while Simon followed more slowly. "I'm happy for you, Mamm," he murmured in her ear. "I know how long you've wanted this."

"How long we've both wanted this." Henry had ears like a cat. He clasped Simon in a brief, hard hug. "I can hardly wait until spring."

Simon went to bed that night with a full heart. As he lay in the darkness, resisting the urge to pull out the mouth organ and play it softly, he wondered if this was the kind of occasion that would compel Cora to make up a song. A song the whole family could sing in sheer celebration.

Because he'd seen that at home in Colorado, Cora would

sing the words and melody she had composed, and her family would make up the harmonies as they went along. It seemed to be a talent the Swareys possessed, because he was pretty sure they were using more than just thirds. All he knew was that whether it was as simple as doing the dishes, or as miraculous as a coming child, they made a joyful noise unto the Lord.

Together.

Dear Father, is it possible that one day it would be Your will that they would include me?

F our more steps and we can turn around." Cora, with Mollie clinging to her arm, made her slow way down the freshly shoveled sidewalk. The Zucker house had two concrete walks—one up to the bakery and around to the outside stairs to the girls' apartment above, and one that ran along the base of the rockery to the downstairs suite. Cora had shoveled them both early this morning, thankful that there hadn't been very much snow last night, and now Mollie was taking her first walk outside.

"I'm deathly afraid of slipping," Mollie confessed, her black scarf tied under her chin even though they were only going to be outside for five minutes. "You won't let me, will you?"

"Not a chance," Cora promised. "Okay, now we'll go back. You're doing very well."

As they made a careful turn, they heard the jingle of harness and the muffled sound of hooves coming along the road. The plow hadn't come along their street yet, but an Amish buggy horse knew its way around snowy streets, as long as the drifts weren't very deep. Behind them, the horse slowed to a stop. It must be a customer for the bakery, though this was the midmorning lull. It was really busy first thing in the morning, when people came to get bread hot out of the oven, and then again at lunchtime, but in between was when the Zuckers got busy in the back with cookie dough and cake batter.

Doors slid open on both sides of the buggy. Cora glanced over her shoulder and stopped in surprise.

Mollie turned, too, and her fingers tightened on Cora's arm. "Dean," she said blankly. "And Simon. Hallo."

"*Guder mariye*, Mollie, Cora." Dean's smile could have melted snow.

Cora hadn't seen Simon in a couple of days. How strange that she still got that shock to her middle when she saw him unexpectedly, like scuffing shoes on a rug and then touching the fridge. When was that going to wear off?

"*Guder mariye,*" she said. "What are you doing here?"

"We're going to the bakery. To find the studs in the wall where the Zuckers want their display rack installed," Simon said.

"I think you might be lost," Cora said dryly.

"Well, Simon here is going to do the measuring, and use the stud finder to figure out where to bolt the rack." Dean lifted a canvas bag that clanked, as though there were tools in it.

"*Neh*, Dean, I think you have that backward," Simon said to him in a low tone that carried perfectly well. "I was going to ask if there was anything the girls needed done downstairs."

If Mollie hadn't been depending on her, Cora might have fallen right over in shock. Simon, offering his time so unselfishly? Simon, who always had better things to do than care for the sick and infirm?

"But it's good experience for you," Dean objected. "Measure twice, cut once, isn't that what you said yesterday? You've used a stud finder, haven't you?"

"*Ja*, but—"

"It's very kind of both of you to think of us," Mollie said, after a glance at Cora. "As a matter of fact, the kitchen faucet has started dripping and the bathtub drains really slowly. I think it's close to being clogged. I've been meaning to ask my *Onkel* to look at it, but ..."

Simon nudged his companion as though this decided it. "Sounds like a job for a washer and a snake. I've fixed both for Mamm, and the Zuckers are waiting on you."

Dean chose the better part and gave in. "I'll come join you all downstairs when you're done," he said.

"In that case," Mollie told them, "maybe you'd like to stay for lunch? We're having bacon and potato soup with grilled cheese sandwiches."

Dean's smile broke out again. "That's the best offer I've had all day."

"*Denki*, Mollie," Simon said. "We'll look forward to it."

Cora could have sworn he nudged Dean toward the upper sidewalk, but maybe it was just her imagination. But once she and Mollie were back inside, she didn't imagine the sound of the shed door opening for a horse, nor of Simon coming into the kitchen door and taking off his boots.

"I think it's warming up," he said cheerfully. "We might even get a melt if we're lucky."

"If it freezes again, that will be the end of my walks to the street," Mollie said.

"At least your pipes aren't frozen," he said. "Let's have a look at this faucet."

The lower suite had probably been remodeled in the sixties

or seventies. The farmhouse sink had the hot tap on one side of the faucet and the cold on the other, with white porcelain handles. The cold tap was the one that dripped. After taking off his coat, Simon got to work, unscrewing the handle and laying it aside, then reaching in to take the guts of it out.

"Cora, do you remember that song you—"

With a gurgle, a fountain of cold water sprayed out of the disassembled tap.

Cora shrieked and grabbed a towel to rescue the pot of soup on the stove next to the sink, but too late. Water had sprayed into it. Water dripped off the counters, the tabletop, the windowsill, and on to the floor.

"Shut it off!" Cora shrieked. "Shut it off!"

"I can't—the valve is out," Simon said. He whipped open the cupboard under the sink. "I forgot to shut the water off first." He burrowed through the contents of the cupboard— trash bucket, cleanser, dish soap, rubber gloves, ant bait, floor detergent—all of it came out on the kitchen floor, to be sprayed with water.

"How much stuff do you have in here, anyway?" His voice rose. "Please don't tell me the shutoff valve is outside."

"My bread!" Mollie wailed, snatching up the loaf of bread waiting to be cut for grilled cheese sandwiches. Its perfectly browned top was soaked.

With a *thunk* from under the sink, the water stopped.

Simon, on his hands and knees under the sink, dropped his head as though in a prayer of thanks. "Inside," he groaned.

"What's going on?"

Cora looked up to see Dean standing in the stairwell that led to the bakery upstairs.

"I heard screaming. Is everyone all right?" His gaze went straight to Mollie. "What happened? You're all wet." He opened drawers until he found the one with the towels and dishcloths in it. He gave Mollie a towel, which she used to dry the bread, then found the box of tissues so she could wipe her face.

"I forgot to turn the water off before I took out the valve assembly," Simon croaked, getting to his feet. "Mollie—Cora—I'm so sorry. I'll clean up the mess."

He was as red as the dishcloth in the sink, and if it were possible to look devastated and horrified at the same time, he did.

"We'll help you," Cora said. She found a potholder and put the soup on the counter. "A little flour will fix the extra liquid in the soup, and Mollie's bread is already dry. Dean, will you walk with her down the hall so she can change clothes? Simon, don't worry about those things from under the sink—we can put them back later. I'll get a mop and have this all cleaned up by the time you get back from the hardware store with the parts."

As if he had remembered what he was there for, Simon pulled up the valve and peeled the ancient washer off. "Cracked," he said. "I'll take it with me. Cora, I'm so sorry. What a *Mopskopp* I am."

"Ischt okay," she told him, mop already in hand as Dean walked with Mollie out to the little hallway where their rooms were. "Anyone can make a mistake. Don't feel stupid—I would never even have thought to turn the water off. Or known where the shutoff was. And now I do." She smiled at him. "We both learned something useful for next time."

Her smile seemed to turn him to stone. Time seemed to slow while her breathing became very loud. His gaze held hers in its molasses grip and the cheery yellow kitchen seemed to fade away at the edges, leaving him at the center, his hair plastered to his scalp and the shoulders of his shirt soaking wet.

The only thing that moved was the drop of water that fell in slow motion off the end of his nose.

She came to herself with a start. "You can't go out like that," she said, and thrust a towel at him. "Dry yourself off. I'll find a muffler for you to wrap up in or you'll catch your death out there."

He snapped out of whatever strange moment that had been, and took the towel. *"Denki,"* came his voice, muffled in its depths.

Thirty minutes later, the washer had been replaced, the kitchen was spotless—Cora had meant to mop the floors and clean the counters today anyway—and everything had been neatly replaced under the sink in the plastic tubs Simon bought along with the washer.

The grilled cheese sandwiches were unharmed by their shower bath, and the soup, Dean vowed after his second bowl, was the best he'd ever had.

"So after all that, we've come out better than when we started," Mollie said with a smile, wearing what looked like a new sage-green dress under her black bib apron. Her hair had been smoothed under a fresh heart-shaped *Kapp*, and there was a color in her cheeks Cora hadn't seen before.

"I could have done without the shower," Simon admitted. "You've been kinder than I deserve, Mollie."

"No harm done," she told him. "And if you come down with a cold, at least Sarah has everything on hand to make you feel better."

"There is that," he said with a chuckle. "Do you always look on the bright side?"

"It's the only side to look on," she said. "When the *gut Gott* puts washers and walkers in our path, it's not to make us miserable, you know. It's to make us thankful that we have water to drink and knees to hold us up and keep us out of the snow."

Simon laughed, and Dean laughed with him.

Later that evening, after Mollie had gone to bed, Cora took out the partially finished quilt that had come in the mail from home and pressed a section of it into the hoop so she could work on the feathers in the borders. Of all the things to happen today, that laugh was what she remembered most. Because the Simon she remembered hadn't laughed like that—with sheer appreciation and good humor. He had smiled, and chuckled, and sometimes laughed in a way targeted to make a point with the listener. Not spontaneously or with honesty.

Her hands, one holding the hoop and the other the needle, lowered to her lap. Was she really analyzing the quality of Simon's laughter? And wondering why there was a difference now when there hadn't been in the spring?

She picked up the needle again. It was a good thing Mamm had sent the quilt so quickly. Because for sure and certain she needed something to do besides think about Simon Yoder.

THE NEXT DAY WAS SUNDAY, the sermon about John the Baptist making the way plain for Jesus' coming. "He wore a coat of skins, and ate locusts and honey," the preacher said. "You wouldn't find the Pharisees dressed so humbly, or eating the fruit of their labor, gained by the sweat of their brow. John was willing to be different, to proclaim Him who was coming after, so that people would see Jesus in all His glory and humility through him."

Simon did his best not to turn his head to look at Cora. He knew exactly where she was sitting—with the young women, a row or two back from Mollie, who had refused a padded chair at the front for her first Sunday back in church after her surgery. Mollie had conceded, though, that she might sit on the end of a row so that if she felt any pain, she could get up and go into one of the bedrooms in the Esch home.

Cora, he had no doubt, would be watching her for the first sign of weariness or discomfort. He would not look to see if his prediction was right. He would keep his eyes on the preacher and listen.

After the service, when the benches and tables had been set up and the fellowship meal set out, he could still see her in the dining room, where the young women sat, from his place with the young men in the big kitchen. He ate his *Bohnesuppe* and bread with peanut butter spread without really tasting them. He visited with his neighbors, who were debating whether or not the volleyball nets would be set up in the barn for a game before supper and the evening singing. Finally the group at his table concluded that since the temperatures had warmed up, probably not.

After lunch, Simon circulated while the women, including his mother, did the dishes. His younger brother Caleb was horsing around with his teenage friends out by the rows of buggies, and Englisch Henry was probably in the barn with the other men, talking about the price of hay and the sermon and whether or not they were likely to get another storm by midweek. But Simon had another objective in mind even while he talked with the *Youngie* and joked and laughed.

But his objective seemed to have disappeared. Back in the house, he strolled through the rooms downstairs, where groups of women visited, the young mothers getting advice from the more experienced ones, rocking their *Bopplin* as they stood, one hip cocked. Where was she?

The dishes were done, and she wasn't in the kitchen. Were the girls all upstairs? He couldn't very well go up and look. He couldn't think of anything more terrifying than walking into a room full of girls and making it completely obvious he was looking for a certain one. That would net him weeks of teasing and embarrass Cora to death.

By pure chance he looked out the window and saw Dean Yutzy leading his horse out into the yard and backing him in between the rails of his no-nonsense buggy. Simon's stomach plunged when he spotted Cora and Mollie crossing the yard toward him.

They were leaving? She wasn't staying for the afternoon and the singing? All his happy plans for the day shredded to pieces and blew away.

In the next moment he was out the door and striding across the yard, now criss-crossed by dozens of buggy tracks. "Leaving so soon?" he called.

Dean was helping Mollie into the front seat, Cora hovering anxiously lest her cousin slip or need an extra hand.

"It's me who is the party pooper," Mollie confessed, her face spasming in pain even as she settled on the bench and smiled at Simon. "But Cora doesn't need to go."

"I'm not going to send you home to be alone while I stay and enjoy myself," Cora exclaimed, her hand on the driver's door, readying to climb into the rear seat. "Dean would never allow it, would you, Dean?" She looked up at him in appeal.

"I'm not sure it's my place to allow anything," he said modestly, "but I have to say I'll be glad to have you along."

Allow anything? Did he mean that he planned to court Cora, and marry her, and have authority over her?

Simon's heart began to gallop, his mind flashing along behind it like a buggy after a racehorse. "But you could come back after you're sure Mollie is comfortable," he said. He glanced at Dean, standing altogether too close to Cora. "Both of you."

A single pleat formed between Cora's finely drawn brows, and was just as quickly smoothed away. *"Neh,"* she said. "I'll be staying home with Mollie. But that doesn't mean Dean can't come back, of course, after he drops us off."

"If you don't mind, I'd like to stay a little while." Dean looked from one young woman to the other. "Just an hour. Not for supper or anything."

"That would be fine," Mollie said. "Or we could just visit out here in the snow, the way we're doing."

Cora laughed. "I think that means let's get moving." She climbed into the back of the buggy, and Dean hopped in beside Mollie.

"Are you coming, too, Simon?" Mollie leaned forward to see him. "I have a new puzzle we could all work on. Five thousand pieces."

The very last thing Simon wanted to do was sort through that many puzzle pieces. Except for the edges, they all looked the same to him. But if Cora was working on a puzzle with Dean, then he'd be at that table, too, no matter the price he had to pay.

"That's very kind of you, Mollie," he said. "I'll hitch up Comet and follow along shortly."

"Cora, you should go with Simon," Mollie said.

"Neh, denki, I'm fine right here," came her muffled voice from the back.

And with that, as though to prevent her changing her

mind, Dean clucked to his horse and the buggy jerked into motion, leaving Simon standing in the snow.

Comet had never been hitched up so quickly in his life. Half an hour later, he was once more putting the horse in the shed behind the bakery, in the stall next to Dean's chestnut, and making sure he had enough hay and a cup of oats as a reward for his patience.

When he knocked on the kitchen door and came into the suite, the first thing he saw was Dean comfortably seated in front of the coffee table in the living room. Mollie was on the sofa under a quilt, her knees elevated and a cup of his mother's steaming summer tea at her elbow. According to the box, the puzzle was of ancient Jerusalem, with people, complicated architecture, a street market, and more animals than a city had any business having in its streets.

But Cora was bringing him a cup of tea, and there was a plate of cake and one of cookies, and puzzle or not, he was staying every bit as long as Dean Yutzy no matter what anyone said.

He settled himself on the fourth side of the table and picked a donkey's nose and mouth out of the pile of pieces.

"It would be fun to put him together," Cora said from behind one of Henry's mugs, "but it's easier to work from the outside in. Like the market awnings in the bottom corner."

Which were red and brown. Easy to pick out. He smiled at her. "Thanks. I don't think I've worked on one of these since I was little. So little that the pieces were made of wood, carved and painted by my father."

"My father made me one like that, too." Dean whisked half a dozen pieces out of the chaos and suddenly the puzzle had a top right corner with a turret or balcony of some kind in it. "I think it was a horse and foal. Or a cow and calf. Dat was no artist, so it could have been one and just looked like the other. But I didn't care. I thought the puzzle was wonderful, and best of all was that he'd made it for me. Not for one of my brothers or sisters."

"Was it a Christmas present?" Mollie asked.

"It must have been," Dean said. "My birthday is in the summer and he wouldn't have had time for carving then."

"Do you still have it?" Cora asked, smiling.

"*Neh*, I think in time it probably went to one of the grand-kids when they visited," Dean told her. "Things like that are meant to be played with, aren't they? Not wrapped in paper and tucked away where a child can't find them."

"*Ja*, I think so, too," Mollie said, color staining her cheeks. Now it was her turn to hide behind her mug.

What was she blushing for? Dean hadn't said anything that remarkable, just a memory from his childhood. Simon found the corner of the market awnings and moved it down to where it might fit at the bottom, then fitted in the red pieces around it. Cora added a couple of brown pieces, and a shadow. Simon hunted for the piece that would connect the red with the brown. It had to be here somewhere. He moved a pile and Cora pounced. "Here!" She snapped it into place and there was a whole corner, done.

"That's all very well, you two, but what about those olive oil jars, there?" Mollie asked. "They're nearly the same color as the street."

You two. Simon savored the words even as he pretended to hunt for pieces of pesky olive oil jars. Hearing those two silly words was nearly as sweet as taking Cora's hand at the top of the stairs at the wedding. Sweeter. At least she was here volun-tarily, not looking as she had that evening, as though she were marching to her own execution.

"It's just you and your brother Caleb in your family, isn't it, Simon?" Mollie asked.

"*Ja*, my father died of the cancer just a few years ago. He and Mamm always wanted a bigger family, but I guess it wasn't *Gottes Wille*." Simon tried to imagine being the eldest of six or seven children without his father. "But considering she was on her own for those years, maybe me and Caleb were enough. I was old enough to look after him when she needed to run the stall at the market, and I did a lot of the heavy work in the garden in the spring."

"And you helped with expenses by working at the buggy shop," Cora put in.

"For a little while." Simon suddenly saw his working life as they must see it—part-time jobs that never lasted very long, working on the ranch but only for the summer, helping out in the pottery but not bringing in actual money for the household.

No wonder Cora had never taken him seriously. For all intents and purposes, he didn't take himself seriously.

"But I'm looking forward to settling in at the blacksmith's and learning a proper trade," he added. "Kelvin seems to be more willing to listen to ideas than ... other men I've worked for."

"He's a *gut* man," Dean said, adding three pieces of the olive oil jars. "There's a lot to learn, though."

"There is in anything worth doing," Mollie pointed out. "Quilting. Cooking. Building houses. No one just walks up to a pile of lumber and starts putting together a house, do they? Even the little boys learn to hammer nails into siding during a barn raising. They have such a small part, but they contribute, and learn by watching the men."

"And the thing about doing something is that you gain

confidence. If I can do this, then maybe I can do that. Like the little boys and their nails." Cora put two pieces of cobbled street next to the market umbrellas, and followed them up with half a chicken.

Simon located the chicken's tail and legs and pressed them into place.

"That was lucky," Cora said. "There have to be twenty chickens in this picture."

"The good thing is they're all different breeds," Simon told her with a smile. "Every one is different, like Mamm's flock. She got the heritage mix order from the hatchery last time."

"I heard a rumor that Sarah and Englisch Henry might be *im e Familye weg*," Mollie said.

Simon stared at her. "Where did you hear that? She just told us two days ago."

Mollie sat back, her brows raised. "Church, Simon. But I am so happy for her, especially if, as you say, she always wanted a larger family."

"Will she give up being *Dokterfraa*, do you think?" Dean asked, hunting for bricks for his tower.

"I don't think she can," Simon said honestly. "It's what *der Herr* and Ruth Lehman willed for her."

Mollie laughed, and then quickly explained to Cora that Ruth had been the old *Dokterfraa* and had turned her practice over to Sarah.

"I have to say she's doing a lot of good in the township," Simon went on. "But people will have to get used to coming to the dispensary at our place more. She probably won't be able to get out to people's houses the way she has been doing, especially in the winter. Not unless it's an emergency."

"Maybe Caleb can do deliveries for her," Cora suggested.

"He has been since he finished eighth grade," Simon said.

"He sure seems to like working with Henry. It wouldn't surprise me if Henry took him on as an apprentice, for actual wages."

He could see good days ahead for his family, leaving the shadows of his father's death and his mother's quiet desperation and grief far behind. "I wasn't certain what to think of Henry when he first came. When he was *Englisch*," he confessed. "We didn't get along so well. But it's different now. Love brought him back to the township when his old *Aendi* left him her farm, and love brought him back to the church when he first laid eyes on my mother."

"That's very wise of you, Simon," Cora said softly. "And God was in both kinds of love, wasn't He?"

There was a faraway look in her eyes. Was she thinking of the two of them, and how good it had been before he'd been so stupid? Or was she thinking of Dean Yutzy, and deliberately not looking at him in case she revealed too much, too soon?

🌾 12 🌾

Dear Hannah,

Thanks for yours. It's pouring rain out here so the logging operation has to shut down for now. At least the seeds and small shoots that might be in the old garden will get a soak, anyway, now that the overstory has been cleared away.

Overstory. That's what they call trees out here.

Rain is a good excuse for cleaning, so I raked out the Airstream and now it's looking pretty good. I even washed the sleeping bags. An hour and it's done. When I think of the hours Mom spends just doing laundry by hand ... even though the washing machine runs on a gas engine, the mangle doesn't, and the clothesline doesn't, and it takes tons of time.

Did you get a chance to look up Devon Perch on the Internet? He said last night at supper (prawns arrabiata, which means enraged prawns in Italian, Callie says ... I'd be enraged too if I was somebody's supper) that the work ethic around here is starting to rub off on him. His agent wants him to do an exhibition, and he says he might just think about it. I guess that's a step in the right direction. Though Devon says thinking exhausts him and he'd rather go surfing.

It's pretty funny to think of my dad and Devon being members of the same species. And here I am, in the middle of two extremes.

Sounds like you're leaning toward the Amish life. I guess I can't blame you. When you were taken away, you lost a whole childhood and teenager-hood. Growing up Amish made me want to be English. Growing up English is making you want to be Amish. Grass is greener and all that, huh? Tell Sam he doesn't know what he's talking about. Anybody can clear land; they don't have to be Amish to do that. Anyways, it's who makes you do it and how you feel when you're done that matters.

It feels good to live in the moment like this, not always with one eye on eternity and letting that affect everything I do. We've only got one life. The Amish look at it like a waystation on the road to better things, but to my mind, that's a waste of a good waystation. I'd rather enjoy every moment now than put them in the heavenly bank for later.

Speaking of living, Callie just came in and invited me to a movie. They have like four theaters in this town, so we ought to find something we both like. The last movie I saw was in Phoenix, with you. I don't even remember the name of it, just that it was cool in the theater and we didn't die of heatstroke like we thought we would. She says we'll go grocery shopping afterward and I can carry everything. If the reward is her cooking I'll carry my own weight in enraged prawns.

Take care of yourself,

Ben

"I t doesn't sound like Ben is coming back, does it?" Cora asked gently. They were sitting on a log on the bank of the frozen pond that filled the dip between the bishop's farm and the Yoder place, watching the boys play hockey. That Tuesday afternoon, it was black knit caps against gray, and gray seemed to be winning, though Cora had lost track somewhere in the middle. Not that it mattered—the *Youngie* didn't play to win. Winning meant someone might feel bad about losing, and causing a bad spirit was something to avoid. Scoring goals was the fun part, not counting how many each side got.

Hannah had told her the gist of Ben's latest letter. In Cora's mind, the news about Ben going on a movie date with Callie was a worry, but Hannah didn't seem aware of it. Or if she was, she was keeping it to herself.

"Not for a while." Hannah sighed. "I specifically told him I was thinking about joining church once I'd got my arms around living Amish. I was hoping he'd tell me what he was thinking."

"Someone who has jumped the fence might not be thinking about going back to the pasture," Cora said. "And what he said about waystations? That's a pretty basic difference in how a person lives—for this world or for the next."

"I know." Hannah watched the black-capped team score, and raised her hands to clap for Dean Yutzy, who had put the puck in the net. "In this world but not of it, right?"

"Right. And being willing for everything that means. Sacrifice. Separation. *Demut und Gehorsamkeit.*"

"Humility and obedience," Hannah repeated. "See? My vocabulary is getting bigger all the time."

"It is," Cora said. "Pretty soon we'll be talking completely in *Deitsch.*"

"And when we do I guess that will be my answer," Hannah said. "At that point I'll know I should quit waffling and start baptism classes."

"I don't think you're waffling," Cora said quietly, shifting on the log and pulling her knitted muffler more closely around her throat. The temperature had warmed up into the forties, and the sky was clouded but not heavy, even allowing the sun to shine through now and again. Still, she'd rather be moving than sitting still. "I think you're coming closer to a decision that probably won't even be a decision. It will just be the next step on a path you're already on."

Hannah got to her feet. "You're so wise. And you might even be right in the end. Come on, let's get some more hot chocolate."

Sallie and her *schweschdere* had set up a table with cookies and brownies, and a big insulated pot full of hot chocolate. She ladled them a cup each, then one for herself, and with a can of whipped cream, made a miniature mountain on the tops of all three. The girls stood together with their mittened hands wrapped around the disposable cups to keep the heat in, watching Simon steal the puck and make a breakaway in the offensive zone.

"The Amish Market has a couple of empty stalls coming open near ours," Sallie said, apropos of nothing.

Hannah cocked an eye in her direction. "*Ja?* And that has what to do with the price of rice?"

Sallie grinned at her. "What funny expressions you use. What it has to do with *you* is that you were talking after church about a coffee stand. And the one thing the Amish Market doesn't have right now is a place to get a decent cup of coffee."

"Oh, I wasn't serious," Hannah said hastily. "That was just dreaming out loud."

"It's another step on the path, though, isn't it?" Cora said to no one in particular, watching the game. "You take steps and find yourself somewhere else. But first you have to actually move your leg and lift your foot to that next place on the path. Like Mollie has to, thinking about every inch of that step."

"All right, Metaphor Girl," Hannah said, "tell us what you really think."

"I think you should rent the stall and make the customers a decent cup of coffee," Cora said simply. "You know how to do that. And you know what equipment you need."

With a sigh, Hannah nodded. "That's the kicker. I do. And it's not cheap."

When she told them what top-end urns and an espresso maker and flavorings might cost, Cora saw why she was giving up on the whole idea before it even began.

"Well, you don't need top end. You could get them used," Sallie said. "You know how to work eBay, don't you? Couldn't you get some things there?"

"If I had to drive a buggy five miles every time I wanted to place a bid, I'd lose every auction," Hannah said. "And I can't ask Dat for that kind of money. I know he hasn't got it."

"What about the Dutch Café?" Sallie said. "Maybe they've got some old equipment in the back they don't know what to do with, and would let you have it cheap."

Hannah blinked. "That's a good idea. I have a little bit saved. They might take it just to free up some space."

"*Gut,*" Sallie said briskly. "I've known the folks who own it my whole life. I'll go with you tomorrow, before the market opens, and we'll ask."

"And if they have something—even if it's just an urn—I'll buy you breakfast."

Sallie laughed. "I'll have had breakfast hours before. But

you can buy me a cinnamon roll. Theirs are almost as good as Mamm's."

Since Hannah didn't yet feel confident enough to harness the horse and take her father's buggy out by herself, Sallie agreed to pick her up the next day at eight thirty. And then the three of them reclaimed the log to watch the last few minutes of the game.

After the goalies skated off, signaling the game was over, the players changed back into snow boots and walked up the slope panting and red-faced. When both grey and black caps streamed toward the hot chocolate and cookies, Sallie took a hasty leave and hurried over to help her sisters with the sudden influx of customers.

Cora dusted the snow off her skirt and she and Hannah joined the crowd. Sallie's younger brother threw some more wood on the bonfire and soon it leaped up, drawing people in toward its warmth. Cora glimpsed Simon on the other side, through the shimmer of heat and smoke. He reached into his jacket pocket for something, and the next thing she knew, a familiar tune rose into the air, punctuated by the popping of wood and a shower of sparks.

A very familiar tune.

"What's the matter?" Hannah whispered. *"Bischt du okay?"*

Around them, a few of the *Youngie* murmured in surprise. Musical instruments, it seemed, were as frowned upon by the *Ordnung* here as they were in Colorado. Even Cora's family, who had been musical for a couple of generations, obeyed the ministers and let their voices be the only music to reach God's ears. But they were on Bishop Troyer's land, and the bishop's children were their hosts. Would someone in authority find out that Simon Yoder had a mouth organ in his pocket and knew how to play it?

Knew how to play one of her songs. How was this even possible?

And what would happen if anyone found out it *was* her song?

He reached the end of the first two lines before he realized that the *Youngie* had fallen silent around him. At the end of the next two lines, one of the boys said, "What's that tune, Yoder? It's not from any of our books."

"Something new from Taylor Swift?" someone else joked, and some of the girls laughed.

But Simon just shook his head in that maddening way he had, smiling like he knew a secret and didn't they just want to know it, too? "You'll never hear it anywhere but here," he said mysteriously. "Except maybe out in Colorado."

"Some band from there?" Sallie's brother asked. "Did you all have a hoedown when you worked at that ranch and a live band played?"

Oh, good grief. This was getting ridiculous. And Simon was enjoying himself far too much. But surely he wouldn't—not in front of—

"Nope," he told them. "You won't hear it anywhere because it's Cora's song."

When would she learn never to put anything past Simon Yoder? Cora wanted to sink into a snowbank and disappear until spring, when just possibly everyone might have forgotten that her face had been so red she could have melted ice against her cheeks.

"What do you mean?" Hannah asked. "Like, Cora made that up?" She turned to gaze at Cora with no little admiration. "I didn't know you wrote music."

"That's because I don't," Cora said flatly. She raised her

voice just enough to carry. "And Simon has no business playing it just to embarrass me."

"I'm not," he yelped, as though she had run a hockey stick into his ribs. "I like the song. I thought you might like to hear it."

"I have heard it," she snapped. "And if I want to hear it again, I'll sing it. But I won't do it in front of a crowd of people, just to draw attention to myself and make a scene."

"But I didn't mean—"

Sure he didn't. He never meant to embarrass her because he never thought things through first. But he did know the fastest way to spoil all their times together, didn't he? He knew how she felt about music, the precious thing she held close to her heart. Her songs were hers alone, meant to be shared only with people she loved and trusted.

Not turned into an attention-seeker's way of getting everyone to look at him and admire his new, forbidden skill on an easily hidden instrument.

"I'm going home," she muttered to Hannah. "Good luck tomorrow, at the café."

"But Cora, the Zucker girls aren't ready to go," Hannah whispered. "After two hours, Samuel just got up the nerve to speak to Dora. Don't make her leave yet."

"I'm not making anyone leave. I said *I* was going." And she'd better move, because tears were clogging her throat. "I'll catch the bus. Mollie has been on her own long enough. It's time I was getting back."

She wrapped her coat around herself as though it would protect her from more than the chilly wind, and walked over the hill in the track that had been tramped flat by a couple of dozen booted feet.

Behind her, the first line of her song rose again, hesitantly, on the air, as though Simon were trying to call her back.

Walk a little while—

But somebody shushed him, and if he tried again, she was too far away to hear.

> Walk a little while, and let Me take your hand
> Walk a little while, and then you'll understand
> Just why I had to come to take your sins away
> Walk a little while—hear what I have to say.

The bus stop was just at the corner a quarter mile from the mouth of the bishop's lane, its plastic and metal forming a shelter against the wind. She hadn't known Hannah when she'd written those words. She'd never sung them to her friend, either, not even when they were doing dishes together and the whole family pitched in. Songs always made the work more fun. And yet, hadn't they been talking about the same subject today, after Hannah had told her about Ben's letter? About walking, and taking steps, every one bringing you closer to a decision and then finally becoming the decision.

Maybe she should change the ending. She tried it out, under her breath.

> Walk a little while, and with each step you'll see,
> Walk a little while, come closer still to Me.
> And with your hand in Mine—"

She hit the joyous high note with a tremolo and the bus

shelter acted as an amplifier, frightening her back down to a whisper.

"—you're on the safest path,
Walk a little while, and home you'll be at last."

"That's beautiful," said a male voice, and Cora nearly jumped out of her skin.

"Simon!"

"You changed the ending." Hands in his pockets, he gazed at her from under the woolly band of his grey knit cap. His brown eyes were contrite. "Did you just make it up? Just now?"

Cora pulled her coat closer. "I'm not talking to you."

He joined her in the bus shelter. On the far side. Small mercies.

"Okay, you don't have to talk. But will you listen? Because I want to apologize."

She gave him her shoulder, leaning out as though to look for the bus. The highway was empty of large vehicles, just the cars of people coming home from work, their headlights like a bright chain down the hill.

"I'm so sorry, Cora. I never meant to embarrass you. I never thought of anything but that you might like to hear your song on an instrument."

"You could have done that in the buggy." The words came out reluctantly. Responding when she'd just said she wasn't talking to him turned her into a liar. "Or in the driveway at Mollie's. Not in front of a crowd—on the bishop's property."

"I guess I could have." He sighed. "I didn't think."

"No, you never do." She turned to face him. "You only think of how things will make *you* feel. It's not about giving me pleasure, it's about showing off in front of the *Youngie*—at my expense!"

His mouth opened, then closed. He tried again. "Is that really what you think?"

"Isn't it the truth?"

"*Neh!* Cora, all I've been trying to do the whole time you've been here is to make you see me differently than you did in Colorado. I'm not the same man I was then."

He would bring that up. The hurt of that final conversation surged through her as though it had just just happened moments ago. "Oh? You've changed so much in six months?"

"I have." He held up a gloved hand and folded down one finger after another. "I've got a job with a future. I burned my hand helping to make the bread rack for the bakery so I could learn faster. I fixed Mollie's faucet and the bathtub drain. I worked on a puzzle—which, believe me, I wouldn't do even for my little cousins when they come to visit."

"Only a selfish person wouldn't lift a hand to give pleasure and companionship to little *Kinner*."

He sighed, gazing at her in dismay. "You're determined to see me as that fool from the summer, aren't you?"

Behind her, the bus's brakes gave a hydraulic hiss as it slowed to a stop. The door opened with a sigh and she climbed the two steps into its steamy warmth.

"I'm not that man anymore," Simon called. The door folded shut and through it, as she tucked her money into the chute, she heard him say, "I'll prove it. I'll be worthy of you. You'll see!"

She fell into the nearest seat on the far side, her face burning, thankful she couldn't see him as the bus pulled away with a roar. An older woman smiled into her bag of groceries. A little blond boy across the aisle whispered, "Mama, why is that

Amish girl so red?" The bus driver glanced into the mirror as though to see for himself what kind of woman could provoke such emotion on a public highway.

Thank goodness they were *Englisch*, and wouldn't have understood what he said.

Still, only Simon Yoder could embarrass her to death twice in one afternoon.

🌿 13 🌿

Dear Ben,

I'm so excited I wish I could just pick up the phone and call you to talk things over. But since my phone is a dead piece of glass and plastic I guess I'll just write fast and pretend we're having a conversation.

Sallie Troyer took me over to the Rose Arbor Inn this morning to talk to the owner. Ginny Hochstetler is a Black woman who used to be Mennonite. You know how you just love some people at first sight? Ginny is like that. She wore earrings shaped like flamingoes and her T-shirt was pink and said, GIRLS JUST WANNA HAVE BUNS with a picture of a cinnamon roll. Oh so true!

We'd tried first at the Dutch Café, but they rent their equipment. So then the owner suggested we try at the Rose Arbor Inn, which was perfect because Priscilla Mast works there and she introduced me.

And now I just realized that I haven't said what's going on and you're probably rolling your eyes at my inability to tell a story in a straight line. Yep, excited. Sallie told me that a couple of single booths are coming open at the Amish Market, and suggested I open a coffee stand. You're probably thinking, well, that's an obvious career choice, but believe me, the thought had never entered my head in any concrete *way. Daydreams don't count. Anyhow, I talked it over with Mom and Dad last night, and to my surprise they thought it was a great idea. Mind you, the market is only open until Valentine's Day, and then they close until May, but it should be long enough to see if this is going to work. It's only a mile from the farm, so unless we have a blizzard, I can walk there every day. Mom says that we could even have a few baked goods to offer people with their coffee, but there are already a few booths selling those so I wouldn't want to step on anyone's toes.*

Anyway—so we get to the Rose Arbor Inn and I mostly coherently make my request, and lo and behold, Ginny says, "As a matter of fact, I was just going to put some old things up on eBay. Come and have a look." She had an old-fashioned twelve-cup urn and wonder of wonders, one of the first espresso machines that De Longhi ever made for US shops. On top of that, it's the same brand that we had in New York, so I can use it blindfolded even though it doesn't have all the bells and whistles. Lucky for me the Market is owned by Mennonite folks (don't tell the tourists) and is wired for electricity, otherwise I'd have to invest in a generator, too.

So between stall rent and equipment and an order for my favorite kinds of coffee beans, I'm basically flat broke. I had to borrow a little from Mom and Dad, but I'll pay them back (I hope) before the Market closes. I had to get a business license, too, but they were really nice in the township office and didn't mind that (a) my NY driver's license was expired and (b) I'm mostly Amish. The fact that the family has been on the farm for like four generations seemed to be more important to them. Now they don't think I'm a flight risk, ha ha.

Did you know that Ginny was engaged to Englisch Henry while he was still English and before he married Sarah? I suppose you would have, your dad being the bishop and all, but I did not. Sallie is full of tidbits like that. She's going to make me a thing something like a table runner, all in pretty Amish colors, to put on the counter of the booth. She's such a sweetheart. I wish I remembered her from when I was little, but I don't. She tells me we sat together in school, but I think I was only enrolled for a couple of months before it happened, and the trauma probably blanked out anything good. Anyway, we're making up for lost time. She sends her love, by the way.

Now all I have to get is a blackboard to write a menu on. And up at the top will be the name of the stall. I'm really going to call it A Cup of Kindness. Because without other people's kindness and my family's love, I would not have a roof over my head, never mind a new little business. It's so exciting. I wish you were here to share it with.

Has Mr. Perch decided to go ahead with the exhibition? Does the car have a new radiator yet? Inquiring minds want to know.

Yours ever,

Hannah

❧

S imon watched the Troyer buggy pass the gate of the smithy again, Sallie at the reins and Hannah Riehl beside her. Word had gone around that Hannah was going to be selling freshly made coffee at the Amish Market, and the general feeling in the *Gmee* was, as his mother had said over breakfast this morning, "That girl is going to take baptism classes in the spring, just you watch."

Simon was happy for her. At least someone's life was looking up, if it couldn't be his, and she had friends like Sallie and Cora to help her.

At the thought of Cora, of her face as she'd turned away and boarded the bus, his heart seemed to squeeze.

"Careful, there." Dean Yutzy handed him his safety glasses. "You forgot these. We use them with the drill press, too."

He knew that. Normally these men didn't have to remind him about the safety procedures; he was doing his best to be vigilant so that those rules would become second nature. But when Cora invaded his thoughts, sometimes she blotted out even his own wellbeing.

"Got something on your mind?" Dean asked. He lowered the spinning bit in the drill press to the clamped metal flange secured in the vise and drilled two neat holes through the marks Simon had made. Four of these would hold the Zuckers' bread display rack to the wall.

Not that you can help with. Though they'd barely spoken to each other at the hockey game, it was driving Simon crazy that Dean was hanging around Cora. Worse, she actually seemed to welcome it. Which was why he hadn't been able to figure out why Dean hadn't immediately gone to hitch up his horse to take her home. His behavior suddenly seemed intolerable to Simon.

"I would like to know something," he said, marking the next clamp.

"I'm listening." Dean took it and put it under the press.

"Why did you let Cora take the bus home yesterday?"

Dean lifted his head to stare at him, and the drill went right through the metal and into the wood base. "Oops." Quickly, he corrected his mistake and moved to the next mark. This small action seemed to allow him to gather his wits. "Why shouldn't she take the bus? She left early so that Mollie wouldn't be alone the whole afternoon."

"*Ja*, I get that, but a man would have taken her home in his buggy."

Dean chuckled and sent the drill through Simon's marking,

then lifted the press easily. "And start another rumor? *Neh, denki.* Once was enough for me. I don't want any more getting in the way."

It was clear that Simon's family wasn't keeping him abreast of the latest on the Amish grapevine. "What rumor?"

"Oh, you know. The one about me courting Cora."

Simon's skin went cold despite the warmth of the smithy. "You are? And yet you let her stand there at the bus stop in the cold while it got dark?"

Dean gazed at him. "Wait. I thought *you* were sweet on Cora. Where was *your* buggy?"

Simon abandoned the clamp and Dean stopped the drill press. "Let me get this straight," Simon said, feeling as though they were going in circles. "You're *not* courting Cora?"

"*Neh,* of course not." Dean's face was flushed, but that could have been from their work and the tint of the safety glasses that rested on his cheekbones. "It's always been Mollie for me, ever since we were children."

Simon felt as though the ice had broken inside him, and a spring creek was swelling up in a rush. "Then how did that rumor get started?"

"The way rumors always do, I suppose. People making assumptions. Cora has been helping me." He sucked both lips in and released them. "I'm not very good at courting. In fact, I'm probably the most inept person there ever was. But as long as Mollie understands my intentions, I don't care what anyone else thinks."

"Well, I'll be." Simon shook his head at himself. "I'll ask your forgiveness, then, for my tone and my words. All this time I thought you were interested in Cora, and it was tearing me up. Not," he admitted quietly, "that you wouldn't be a good husband to her ... or any woman."

"I don't want any woman. I want Mollie. I always have. And I believe the *gut Gott* brought me back here to see if she wants me, too."

Feeling as though a burden had been carried off his shoulders by that spring rush of relief, he marked the third clamp and handed it to Dean.

He took it and eyed Simon before he started up the press once more. "So then your attempt to recreate Noah's flood in Mollie's kitchen was so you could do something for them? For Cora?"

Simon nodded. "But everything I try just seems to make it worse. Yesterday it was the same. I played one of her songs thinking it would please her, and she got so angry that she left early."

"She wasn't angry," Dean said. "Just embarrassed."

"But I didn't mean to embarrass her." Simon's shoulders slumped. "How can I prove I'm not the selfish *Zwickel* she thinks I am when everything I try goes wrong?"

"You fixed the faucet," Dean pointed out. "Eventually. And the tub."

"*Ja*, but not before making things worse than they were to start with."

"I'm sure Noah went through the same when he was building the ark. He didn't know he'd succeeded, though, until the water lifted him up. Closer to God."

Simon tilted his head to gaze at his companion. *Closer to God.*

Dean might be hopeless at courting, but he seemed to be pretty wise in other ways. Simon said no more, just picked up and marked the last clamp, and they went back to work.

But that night, after dinner, his family settled in the sitting room for their round-robin reading of their nightly chapter of the Bible. They were in the Psalms, and in her sweet, soft voice, Sarah read, *"But it is good for me to draw near to God: I have put my trust in the Lord God, that I may declare all thy works."*

The words wouldn't leave him. Later, Simon went upstairs and sat on the quilt that covered his bed, made by his mother from pieces cut from shirts he and Caleb had long outgrown.

Closer to God.

Was *der Herr* trying to tell him something? Was that why nothing was working? He knew as well as any of the *Youngie* that the right way to find your life's partner was to leave the choice in God's hands. He had planned which of His children were right for each other from the beginning, and it was up to each one to put him or herself in that comforting hand. It was only when a person took their own way, did things on their own, that trouble ensued.

Was that what he'd done? Oh, sure, he said his prayers every night. Mamm had brought them both up to come to God at the beginning and end of the day, though she no longer came in to kneel by the bed and hear their little prayers together.

But Simon realized even as he stared at the hooked rug he had been kneeling on for half his life, that he had been saying the prayers of a child. Repeating words he had been taught because it was easy and he thought he was doing both his mother's and God's will.

But now he was a man, and in dire need of the kind of guidance that only sincere and honest prayers could bring.

When I was a child, I spake as a child, I understood as a child, I thought as a child: but when I became a man, I put away childish things.

Paul had said that. Had he gone through this, too? He must have—and more, too, on that road to Damascus.

Simon slid off the bed and knelt on the rug, his face buried in his hands.

Lord, I come to you—long after I should have—to ask your forgiveness. I have been blind, and I have hurt people—the Gundersons, Cora, my mother—in my blindness. Please forgive me. Please pick me up and set me on the road you want me to walk, because I can't find it for myself.

Lord, I don't deserve Cora. I don't deserve her, because I haven't asked you if caring for her is your will for me. I'm asking now, Lord. Please reveal your will to me, and if she is the partner you want for me, I'll give thanks on my knees every day of my life. But if she's not, and you have a better man in mind for her, help me to bear it. To be a brother to her, to give unselfishly. Oh Lord, I don't even know how to do anything unselfishly. Help thou mine unbelief. Help thou my self-centeredness.

Help me to put you at the center. I know everything else will fall into place. Thank you for what you've put in my life already. Thank you for my mother, and Henry, and Caleb, who love me even though I'm unworthy. Thank you for my little brother or sister coming in the spring. Thank you for Kelvin, and Dean, who has shown himself to be a friend in disguise. Help me to fit better into the Gmee, to find my place and love it simply because you want me there.

Thank you for loving me, Lord. Amen.

When Simon got to his feet and climbed into bed, he could almost feel the last chunks of ice that had been holding him fast swirling away on the current inside him. And when he lifted his hand to his face, it came away wet with tears.

❄ 14 ❄

Dora Zucker clattered down the bakery's back stairs and poked her head into the kitchen. "Mollie—Cora—telephone for you."

Mollie, seated at the table rolling pie pastry, looked up. "Cora, can you go? I'm covered in flour."

Dora laughed. "You'd fit right in. But it's all right. It's the *Dokterfraa* and she asked for either one of you."

Cora ran up the steps and emerged into the bakery's big commercial kitchen. The telephone hung on the wall by the door, its receiver lying on the counter.

"Hallo, Sarah," she said. *"Wie geht's?"*

"Very well, *denki,"* the *Dokterfraa* replied. "How is Mollie?"

"She's doing well, too. The doctor at the county hospital wants to see her next week for a checkup, but she's doing everything he asked so he should be happy with what he finds."

"Ah, *gut,* I'm glad to hear that. Has she found any of the cures I sent over to be helpful?"

Cora smiled, and it carried over into her voice. "She has,

for sure and certain. The pain in her hands is down by half, she says, because of avoiding nightshade. The summer tea helps when she feels discouraged or in pain, and the green salve is working wonders on the surgical sites. I thought nothing worked better than Burn & Wound, but this must be something special."

"It is," Sarah said, sounding pleased. "Well, this is good news. But I have another reason for calling. Since Mollie is doing so well, would the two of you be free for dinner this evening? I went by your aunt and uncle's earlier, and they're planning to come, so I thought you might like to, as well."

How kind she was! "We would," Cora said promptly, without even checking with her cousin. "What time?"

"Best to come a little early, since we don't know what the weather is going to do. Old Joe Yoder says his ankle feels snow, but Simon says the forecast on the radio at the auto shop next to them was only for clouds."

Cora felt the jolt right under her heart at hearing Simon's name. Which was silly, considering she was talking to his mother and of course his name would come up.

"Who do you believe?" Cora asked, laughing to cover up the tiny hesitation.

"Honestly?" Sarah dropped her tone. "Old Joe's ankle has been pretty reliable. I wouldn't discount it—which is why I'm suggesting you come a little earlier."

"We'll be there," Cora promised. "We're baking raisin pies today—shall I bring a couple along?"

"That's Henry's favorite," Sarah said. *"Wunderbaar."*

So, almost on the dot of five, Cora guided the Zucker buggy into Englisch Henry and Sarah's yard. The Zuckers weren't going out tonight, so they'd pressed the buggy on them so that Mollie wouldn't have to brave the bus with

Cora, or try to fit comfortably into the back of their uncle's buggy.

A familiar tall shape detached itself from the shadows at the end of the porch.

"Guder owed," Simon greeted them as he came over to put a hand on the horse's harness. "Let me put your horse up. Your aunt and uncle just got here."

"Denki, Simon," Mollie said as Cora helped her down.

"Yes, thank you," Cora said softly. She could have put the horse in the barn herself, but it was a gesture of kindness and hospitality for a young man of the household to do so. Besides, her biggest concern was for Mollie and getting her up the steps and inside.

Sarah welcomed them at the door, her grey eyes looking Mollie over as though checking that she was all right. Thank goodness the *Dokterfraa* could only see the injuries of the body. The ones in the heart weren't so easily diagnosed or treated— though Cora had heard that Sarah Byler was pretty good at that, too.

She and Mollie greeted their aunt and uncle in the spacious living room.

"Your three weeks is about up, isn't it, Cora?" Onkel Jeremiah said as she settled on the sofa next to Aendi Kate. "Mollie, what do you say? Will she be heading home soon?"

"I hope not," Mollie said with a smile, walking slowly over to a chair unassisted. "I'm doing pretty well. Except for the steps up to the bakery and harnessing the horse on my own, I can do far more than I could before the surgery. I'm just taking it slower, that's all."

"I'm glad to hear it," their uncle said. "You'd let us know if you needed a ride anywhere, or anything done around the house, *nix?*"

"*Ja, Onkel,*" Mollie said with affection. "People have been wonderful. The Zucker girls take me to church, and Simon and Dean have been over to do repairs."

"I heard about that," came from the kitchen, where Sarah was putting the final touches on dinner with Caleb's help.

"I heard that Simon made a geyser in the kitchen sink," Caleb said.

"No fair telling stories on him when he's not here," Cora called.

"Oh, he told us the story, never fear," Sarah said with a laugh as Simon came through the back door in time to hear. "On the good side, it won't happen in this kitchen, he says, because now he knows to turn the water off before he starts work."

Onkel Jeremiah guffawed, and as Sarah called them all in to dinner, he clapped Simon on the back. "Every experience is a learning experience, *nix?*"

"I'd say so," Simon said, his good humor not affected a bit by the teasing. "Whether we come out of it smiling or not. At least it makes a good story for little brothers to tell."

If Cora had thought that dinner might be awkward, or Simon might find a way to embarrass her, she found that by the time Sarah served up their raisin pie she was mistaken. In actual fact, she'd never seen Simon so considerate. Instead of drawing attention to himself, as he might have done when the talk turned to work, he deflected the conversation to Dean and how much he was learning from him.

Mollie seemed particularly interested in that, and Cora noticed that Simon took care to talk not only about what Dean was teaching him, but how he was doing so.

"He's orderly, and I like that," he said, not seeming to notice that Mollie was following every word the way the girls in Colorado used to—only for much sillier reasons. "When you're a novice like me, every step matters. Dean doesn't leave out the little things I need to know."

"Maybe because it hasn't been all that long since he learned them," Onkel Jeremiah observed.

"Maybe not," Simon acknowledged, "though he apprenticed in Mifflin County, where he lived before. I think he's pretty experienced. I wouldn't be surprised if Kelvin asks him to be partner some day. Kelvin's *Kinner* are still scholars, so it will be a while before his eldest can apprentice with him, if that's what he wants."

Mollie sat back, a blush on her cheeks, as though Simon had complimented her and not the absent Dean.

When they'd finished dinner, Cora said to Sarah, "I never knew Hungarian *goulasch* could be so good. What's the secret?"

Sarah laughed. "Henry likes a heavy hand on the paprika, but I find using red peppers instead of green really makes a difference. And homemade noodles, of course. The ones from the bulk store just don't taste the same, do they?"

"*Neh*, they sure don't. Let me and the boys do the dishes, Sarah. You've worked hard enough today."

Cora shooed her into the living room and addressed herself to the stack of dishes. Caleb took up his station with the dish towel, while Simon used one of the double sinks to scrub plates and pots before she took them on the soapy side.

Caleb began to sing—a familiar song her own mother had taught them to make doing dishes more fun. It was called "Who Built the Ark?" and even Simon laughed and answered the question using a different voice every time. Mollie, who was putting the dishes away—and getting practice stretching her knees—joined in on the chorus as though they were all still scholars.

When they wound it up, and a couple of other songs from the little handwritten songbook lying open on the windowsill, they hadn't got through the pots yet. "Do you know 'The Faithful Carpenter'?" Simon asked.

Cora caught her breath. After being so great all evening, he wasn't really going to do this, was he? And spoil it all?

"No, how does it go?" Mollie asked.

"Here's the first verse," Simon said. "I bet you can figure out the line where everyone joins in."

> The carpenter is standing
> On a barren plot of ground
> But in his mind the house is complete and new.
> He uses all his years of skill
> To make the foundation sound
> Look up, carpenter,
> The walls must be straight and true.

"Oh, I like that," Mollie said. "What's comes next?"

Cora gave in to the inevitable, and joined Simon for the second verse. Which she knew by heart—because both words and tune had come from her heart.

> He's labored all his life
> To build a house unseen
> Its walls are strong, its rooms are filled with
>   love.
> He invites his Lord to dwell there
> Whatever cost it means
> Look up, carpenter,
> And peace will come from above.

Now he stands in that great doorway
That leads to heaven and home
He sees the roofs of those heavenly mansions
    fair
His journey now is ended
No more on earth to roam
Look up, carpenter,
The Savior awaits you there.

"Ach, that's wonderful *gut*," Sarah said. "Please, Simon, can you write that out in my *Liederbuch*?"

Simon glanced at Cora, almost as though he were asking permission. When she gave a barely perceptible nod, she realized he wasn't going to embarrass her by announcing who had composed it—instead, he'd simply do as she asked and let Cora say so if she wanted to.

"Isn't that one of yours, Cora?" Aendi Kate asked from the living room. "I believe we sang it at your parents' place the summer before last—and you wrote it into my songbook before we went home."

Well, so much for that.

Sarah's eyes were wide. "*Ischt so*, Cora?"

Before she could reply, Englisch Henry said with appreciation, "What a gift *der Herr* has given you—and us."

Sarah looked as though she'd just had an idea. "Maybe ... well, could I ask you to write it out for me? That way it would be in your own handwriting, a little souvenir of this evening."

How could she say no? After all the care Sarah had taken of Mollie, surely she could do this little thing for her in return. "As soon as we get these dishes done, I will."

She caught Simon's eye as she turned back to the sink, and he made a rueful face. It was gone in an instant, but she understood. He'd tried, but there was no accounting for relatives!

While Caleb wiped down the counters, Simon found her a pen and turned his mother's book to a fresh page. Carefully, she began to write out the words that had come to her one day after church, when they'd driven past a half-completed house.

When she was finished, she put the songbook back on the windowsill and joined her family in the living room. To her surprise, Aendi Kate was already hunting for her handbag—a sure sign that they would be leaving soon.

"Going already, Onkel?" she asked with a glance at her cousin. "Mollie, are you ready to go, too?"

"It wouldn't hurt." Mollie moved the drape aside to look out into the yard. "Looks like Old Joe Yoder's ankle was right after all. It's snowing."

Amid the flurry of leave-taking and locating coats and boots, Simon and Caleb went out to help Onkel Jeremiah harness the horses.

"I'm glad you were able to come, you two," Sarah said as Cora and Mollie put on their coats and wound scarves around their necks. "Mollie, you're moving so much more comfortably now."

"I am," Mollie said, clearly pleased that the *Dokterfraa* had been able to see it. "Onkel Jeremiah is right—Cora should be thinking about her own life, and making plans to get home. I can get along much better now."

"Do you want to get rid of me that bad?" Cora said with a laugh. "And here I thought you *liked* my cooking."

"I do," Mollie told her. "But you have a life and a home, and I don't feel completely right about keeping you away from either one."

Out the kitchen window, Cora could see Simon leading

Onkel Jeremiah's horse through the barn doors, hitched up to the buggy with the lamps already lit. The snow was over the wheel rims already, blurring the ruts in the yard into smoothness and making it look as though company had not come at all. Jeremiah helped Aendi Kate into the buggy, and with a wave, climbed in and shook the reins over the horse's back. It set off at a brisk clip that no doubt their uncle would keep up until he got his wife safely home.

In a few moments, Simon led out the Zucker horse and buggy, its lamps already lit, too. Cora turned to Sarah and Henry. "Thank you so much for inviting us. It has been wonderful *gut*."

"And your song made it special," Sarah said in a low voice. "Thank you for sharing it with us."

"Simon did the sharing," she had to confess. "It was a surprise to me that he remembered it."

"At least it was only with his family and ours," Mollie pointed out. "Thank you so much, Sarah and Henry. *Kumm*, Cora. We don't want the poor horse all covered in snow." She set off by herself.

Sarah frowned, and took a half step after her.

But Mollie made it down the stairs and to the walk without trouble, her hand lying lightly on the stair railing. Tying the ribbons of her away bonnet as she followed her down the steps, Cora watched carefully as Mollie crossed the yard toward Simon. She was walking as confidently as she used to before her knees had made it necessary to use the walker. Was that why her pace looked so quick?

"Mollie, wait," Cora called, abandoning her ribbons and hurrying down the walk. "Watch out for—"

Simon came around by the horse's head, clearly having

heard the concern in her voice. Mollie looked up from where she was going, distracted for just a second.

Just long enough for her toe to catch in one of the hidden ruts and send her headlong into the snow.

"Mollie!" Cora shrieked, and dashed across the yard.

Lying facedown, Mollie did not move. Cora flung herself to her knees next to her cousin, horrified to see that from her nose there came a tiny trickle of blood.

❧ 15 ❧

Lay her on the bed," Sarah said urgently to her husband. He did so, as gently as though Mollie were made of unfired greenware. To Cora, she said, "Get her boots and bonnet off while I make up a compress for her nose. She landed flat on her face."

"I should never have let her go marching off alone." Cora was near tears as she pulled off Mollie's boots.

"I'b fide," Mollie insisted, tugging at the knot in her away bonnet's black ribbons with one hand as she held a handkerchief to her nose with the other.

"You are *not* fine," Cora told her. "You measured your length on frozen ruts and for all we know your nose could be broken."

"You scared me to death." Simon's face looked white as he hovered in the bedroom doorway. "I was never so glad to see anything as when you opened your eyes."

"Simon, come with me," Henry said, heading for the door. "We'll put the horse up for the night and let your mother do her good work."

"Whud?" Mollie exclaimed.

"But—" Cora said in the same moment.

"Never you mind," Henry said, as sternly as his gentle, diffident character would allow. "Sarah will never allow you to go home. Not when there might be complications."

"Right!" the *Dokterfraa* called from her compiling room across the hall. "I want to keep an eye on you overnight, Mollie. We'll talk in the morning."

"But—" both Cora and Mollie said at once.

"No buts." Henry smiled at them. "I'll leave a message at the bakery or for sure and certain we'll have all three Zuckers over here wondering what's become of you—and their buggy."

Cora's gaze met that of her cousin as the men left the room. "I guess we'd better do as we're told," she said.

Spend the night in Simon's home after all this effort she'd spent trying to convince herself she felt nothing? It was *gut* that she'd be watching Mollie. Because there was not much hope of sleep under these circumstances.

"Awkward," Mollie murmured.

"Don't think about it," Cora whispered back. "I'm trying not to."

As gently as she could, she removed Mollie's away bonnet and *Kapp* and hung them from one of the pegs. Then she found a couple of cushions from the sofa and slipped them under her cousin's knees.

"That feels better," Mollie sighed. "And I was doing so well, too."

"It is the third week," Cora pointed out. "Dean warned us, didn't he?"

Mollie touched her nose gingerly. "Don't remind me ... because you know he will."

Sarah bustled in with a bag of crushed ice and a pot of

salve. "Hold this to your nose and let's get your tights off. I want a look at those knees. I hate to say it, but better you landed on your hands and face than on your knees."

Mollie groaned and wordlessly put the ice to her face, where even now Cora could see bruises forming.

"Do you think it's broken?" Cora asked anxiously as she removed Mollie's warm black tights, which all the females in the township wore in the winter.

"I'll check in a minute, but let's stop the swelling first," Sarah said, looking closely at Mollie's knees. "These look good, *Liewi*. A little salve and then we'll get you into one of my nightgowns."

"Ohgay," came her plugged-up voice from behind the bag of ice.

To Cora's intense relief, half an hour later Sarah declared that the nose was not broken, and on top of that, Mollie's pupils behaved as pupils were supposed to, which meant that she hadn't suffered a concussion.

Sarah nodded with satisfaction. "A cup of a special tea I have brewing on the stove and you'll be able to sleep." She glanced at Cora. "Both of you. The bed is big enough for two, and I have more than one spare nightie."

"*Denki*, Sarah," Cora said gratefully.

So in the time it would have taken for them to drive home, only to worry for the rest of the night, Cora found herself tucked up next to her cousin, both of them with hot cups of tea in their hands that smelled like daisies and peaceful gardens. Simon and Caleb both came in through the kitchen door, and they could hear their mother refusing to let either of them look in to say good night.

"It isn't proper," she said firmly.

But that didn't stop a quiet voice from coming down the

hallway. "*Guder nacht*, Mollie," Simon said. "I'm glad you're going to be all right."

"*Guder nacht*, Simon," Mollie said, relaxing into the pillows.

"Sleep well, Cora," he said in an even softer tone. "Don't worry about anything. We'll look after you."

"*Guder nacht*," Cora managed around the sudden, unexpected lump in her throat. She swallowed it down with a gulp of tea.

In lieu of their nightly Bible reading, the Byler family said their prayers together in the living room, just loudly enough for Cora and Mollie to hear that they had been included in the family's petitions to Heaven.

Just loudly enough for Cora to hear Simon praying for her.

She opened her eyes after saying her own prayers when she heard the sounds of the family going up to bed, and in the dimness of the lamp they hadn't yet extinguished, saw that Mollie had turned her head on the pillow and was watching her, her eyelids drooping with weariness.

"I've never seen Simon Yoder like this," her cousin said softly, so that her words wouldn't go beyond the bedroom door of the old farmhouse. "He seems ... different. Changed."

"He's at home, not out in public making a spectacle of himself."

"Is it because of you?"

"*Neh.* It's not my job to change him, Mollie."

"Maybe not." Her cousin yawned. "But I think it's happening all the same. Or haven't you noticed?"

By the time Cora found the words for a reply, Mollie's eyes had closed and her body had gone limp as she slid into sleep. Gently, Cora took the mug Henry had made from her cousin's unresisting fingers and put them both on the night table.

She had noticed. But Cora didn't have any faith in a man's

ability to change himself. That was entirely the good Lord's business, and she would be long gone back to Colorado before anyone saw the proof in *that* particular pudding.

❦

THE GOOD THING about being the son of the *Dokterfraa* was that he understood that a body needed sleep after a stressful event—even young, healthy bodies. So no one in Sarah's household gave another thought to allowing Mollie and Cora to sleep through breakfast. The downside, though, was that Simon didn't get to see Cora before he had to leave for work.

But just thinking of her tucked up under Mamm's quilts made him feel warm inside. Was this how Henry felt to know that his wife was safe under a roof he had provided? Would Simon ever know that privilege with Cora?

Something had changed between them last night, and not because of the scare with Mollie. It had been over her song. Instead of being the one to announce that she had composed it, he had stifled his urge and in the spirit of *Uffgeva*, given place to her. The fact that her aunt had then taken her choice away wasn't the point. And it had all turned out all right— keeping it in the family.

Oh, how he wanted her to be his, and thus part of his family!

"Do you think she'll change her plans to go back to Colorado now that Mollie needs her for a little while longer?" he asked Comet as they made their way into Whinburg, the sound of his hooves muffled by the fresh snow. "I've still got time to show her I've changed, don't I—that I'll put her first in all things if she'll only give me another chance?"

But Comet, usually so understanding, just flicked an ear in

annoyance as he picked his way across the smithy yard to the barn. The horse might be a good listener, but when the footing was uncertain he clearly didn't like to be distracted.

Simon stepped around Kelvin's horse, harnessed to the cargo wagon waiting in the shop doorway to find Kelvin and Dean wrapping the completed bread display rack in old blankets for the trip over to the bakery.

"Have trouble getting through the snow?" Kelvin asked, his way of saying, *You're late.*

"No," Simon said, shrugging out of his coat. "We had a little excitement last night when Mollie Graber fell, and she stayed the night with us. Things were a bit disorganized this morning." He wasn't about to say that he'd hung around the house until the last possible moment, hoping Cora would be up before he left.

"Mollie fell?" Dean dropped the blanket and had to make a grab for his end of the rack before it tilted. "What happened? Is she all right?"

Simon took pity on the poor guy and kept the story brief and positive. But still, Dean's face had paled with distress.

"You're sure she's okay?" he said, then clutched at his black hat. "It's the third week. I knew it. The third week will get you every time."

"Luckily she'd come to dinner at our house, and my mother had a bag of ice on her nose and the rest of her in bed with her knees elevated within minutes. She wouldn't let them go home."

"That was wise." Dean didn't look much comforted, though. "If only we were married, I could look after her myself."

Kelvin's eyebrows rose up under the brim of his own hat. "So that's how it is, eh? What's stopping you?"

Simon never knew whether Kelvin was joking or not, but this didn't seem to be a joke.

"I—I—" Dean halted. "Well ... nothing." He said it as though it were a revelation, as though he'd never considered it before. Which Simon knew perfectly well wasn't true—Dean thought about Mollie all the time. But sometimes maybe all a man needed was a little nudge out of his paralysis to get him going in the right direction.

"We're going right to their house," Simon pointed out. "Mollie will be home by the time we've finished the installation in the bakery. Kelvin won't mind if we drop in to see how she is, will you?" He appealed to their employer.

Kelvin appealed to *Himmel* for a brief moment, as though asking what he had done to deserve two employees who were both of a mind for courting. "*Ja*, all right," he said at last. "I suppose ten minutes won't hurt."

"Ten minutes!" Dean yelped.

Kelvin only shook his head and with a jerk of his chin, indicated that they should heft the swaddled rack into the back of the wagon. "I didn't borrow my brother's Percheron to keep him standing around waiting for you two."

Ten minutes wasn't much. But Simon knew better than anyone that ten minutes could change the course of your whole life. Now he just had to put his energy and brain power into changing his own. As soon as *der Herr* revealed to him where He wanted it to go.

The bakery was in the middle of its morning rush, but that didn't stop the Zucker sisters from temporarily abandoning the crowd in line to buy bread and muffins to get their first glimpse of the new bread rack. Sam Riehl, on his way up the steps, helped them carry the awkward piece inside, and give

Simon a hand holding it in place while Kelvin bolted it to the wall.

"Oh, isn't it beautiful," Karina, the middle sister, said with a sigh. "It's just perfect."

"Not quite," Simon confessed at a glance from Kelvin. That spot where he'd lost his concentration on the twist probably couldn't be seen by anyone but himself and Kelvin, but still, he couldn't let the new owner believe it was perfect.

"No, don't tell me," she said, holding up a hand. "Even if it's not perfect, a little blemish keeps us humble, doesn't it?"

Someone in line cleared their throat, and the two elder sisters went back to work. "Bread," Dora said urgently. "Simon? Samuel? Help me load the bread on our beautiful new shelves."

While Kelvin picked up the blankets and his toolbox and took them out to the wagon, Simon and Sam did as they were commanded. It wasn't until they had the rack half loaded and Simon was practically swooning from the smell of fresh, warm bread that he realized Dean had disappeared.

He smothered a smile. *Good for you, Dean. Seize your opportunities when God sends them.*

CORA HAD NEVER SEEN Dean so agitated. She ushered him into their little living room, where Mollie had just got settled, and went into the kitchen to make tea and take off her coat and away bonnet. She heard the murmur of voices start up right away. So, tucking a stray strand of hair back into her *Kapp*, she found a kitchen apron and rinsed out the teapot.

At which point she was frozen in place by the clarity of Dean's voice.

"I know it's sudden—and of course you'll want time to think it over—but Mollie, I can't wait another minute. Will you make me the happiest man in Lancaster County and agree to be my wife?"

In slow motion, Cora set the teapot on the counter before her nerveless fingers dropped it. What should she do? Go into her room? But they'd see her and it would spoil a moment that was not designed for three. Oh dear. Cora hardly dared to breathe.

"Does this have something to do with my falling in the snow last night?" Mollie's voice was cool and clear, and it didn't sound like she minded if Cora heard.

Or maybe she'd forgotten Cora was there. Cora would have, in her place.

"*Neh*, of course not." A pause. "Well, maybe a little. I just realized that if I had been with you, maybe it wouldn't have happened."

"My cousin was with me, and it happened anyway. It was a silly accident, because it's week three. There's no reason for you to get all het up about it."

He made a sound halfway between a laugh and a gasp. "There's a very good reason."

"Because you think I can't look after myself?" Mollie asked. "That I'm an invalid?"

"If anyone can look after herself, it's you," he said. "I just want to be by your side, Mollie, from week three to however long the *gut Gott* gives us. I want to fix your sink, and kiss you good-bye in the morning, and provide for you, and make a home with you. I—I know that you've suffered losses, but I hoped that maybe you might still want those things, too. With me."

Mollie's independent streak was a mile wide. But oh, Cora

thought, who could resist such kind eyes? *Come on Mollie, say yes and put the poor man out of his misery.*

"There is something to be said for a man who can fix a sink without flooding the whole house," her cousin finally allowed.

"Does that mean—?" Cora could picture his eyes searching her face, hoping ...

"*Ja,*" Mollie said with a sob as her composure broke in a million pieces. "*Ja,* for sure and certain I'll marry you. After waiting half my life for you, let's make it soon!"

Cora covered her mouth with both hands to hold back both laughter and tears. Blindly, belatedly, she pulled her coat off the hook by the door and slipped outside to give them some privacy.

And walked straight into Simon Yoder's arms.

❧ 16 ❧

"Oh!" Cora landed in Simon's arms as though she'd been pushed. Forgotten, the shovel he'd been using fell into the snow as, instinctively, his arms folded around her.

Since he'd felt like a third wheel upstairs, he'd left Sam Riehl to finish loading the bread rack with Dora. He'd planned to shovel off the walks and had been about to begin with Mollie's back porch, when Cora had barreled into him.

"Careful," he said gently. *Just give me one second to marvel at how right she feels*, he prayed. *Just one.*

That was about all he got. One second.

"I'm so sorry," she choked, and pushed away. "But Mollie —Dean, he—"

"I figured he'd gone downstairs," Simon said easily, and bent to pick up the shovel. "I was just going to clear your walks."

"Simon, he's *proposing*!"

Simon grinned. "When he makes up his mind, he doesn't waste any time. Come on, let's give them a couple of minutes."

"That's what I was *doing* when you—"

"When I?" He cleared the three cement steps and started on the short walk that ended at the small barn behind the bakery. The Percheron waited patiently for them to remember when it was time to leave.

"When you caught me," she said primly. "You missed a spot." She pointed.

He picked up the three inches of loose snow and tossed them to one side. "Good for Dean, I say. He was pretty upset about her falling last night. I'm glad he's not wasting any time."

"You're glad?" She slipped her bare hands into her sleeves and hugged them against her middle. "I thought you didn't like him."

"I didn't, at first," he admitted, the shovel scraping with an efficient rhythm across the concrete path. She moved with him down the clean walk. "But that was because I thought he was courting you."

She snorted. "You and half the township. Honestly, I don't even live here. Why was everyone so set on matching me up?"

"You know the Amish grapevine." A few more scoops of the shovel and the walk was done. "I'll clear the front. Though I might spoil the moment if they see me through the window."

"I don't think an earthquake would spoil their moment," Cora said, following him around the side of the house. "I'm so happy for Mollie. The grapevine will have a field day now, thinking Dean dumped me in favor of her."

"No one in his right mind would dump you," Simon said, meaning it.

"You did."

He felt the cut right to his heart, as though her words had done physical harm.

Again, he realized how it must have felt when he'd said what he did in Colorado. He'd been so careless. So unfeeling.

No wonder she had kept her distance ever since. He'd apologized, but now he wondered if that was enough.

"Cora, I'm so sorry for what I said then. I was an idiot."

"*Ja,*" she agreed pleasantly.

"I understand now how you must have felt."

"Do you?" She wasn't giving an inch.

He nodded. "But there's no point in trying to go back and rewrite the past. What I need to do is to just wait. For *der Herr* to tell me what He wants." He dug the shovel into the trampled snow on the top step of the bakery's wide, welcoming front porch. "That was my mistake."

"Since I've been here, that's the first thing you've said that I've agreed with." Her tone was thoughtful.

"I've been praying," he said. What if she didn't believe him?

It wasn't until he'd reached the third step that she spoke. "I'm glad."

Only two words, spoken softly, but no treasure could have had more value.

He didn't dare say more in case his tongue got ahead of his heart and spoiled it. So he simply worked his way down the broad plank steps of the old house, removing the layer of trampled snow. And when Cora fetched a broom to sweep them completely clean, revealing their white planks once again, he had to tell himself not to do something crazy, like break into song. Only the bakery customers picking their way down the steps kept him quiet.

Because it had been a long, long time since he and Cora had done something together so spontaneously, the way they had in the beginning. Then, it had seemed so natural for him to pitch in and help her weed the garden, or for her to save him a slice of his favorite pie after church. To take complementary parts at singing, each supporting the other.

Helping each other, not because they had to, but because they wanted to be together and any reason was a good one. It didn't matter what they were doing. It was the *together* part that counted.

Could this be our first baby step toward that togetherness again? Is this a sign from you, Lord, showing us the way we should go?

But the Lord didn't answer him. He had, however, put Simon right where the opportunity presented itself, hadn't he, when Cora had practically fallen out the back door? Bless Dean Yutzy for being in such a rush to propose!

Speaking of which ...

The jingle of harness came from behind the house, and in a moment the Percheron, with Kelvin at the reins, drew level with Simon and Cora, who by then were about halfway down the front walk with shovel and broom.

"Any chance my journeymen will be getting back to their actual jobs soon?" he inquired, his forearms on his knees and the reins loose in his hands. Even the Percheron gave Simon a reproachful look.

"Dean—he—" Cora turned to Simon in appeal.

"Dean is in there proposing to Mollie Graber," Simon said in a confidential tone. "We're giving them some privacy."

"Lucky it's not below zero," Kelvin said. "Well, come on if you want a ride back. Dean can get a ride with someone else, or take the bus."

But somehow Dean must have heard the Percheron moving out, for the front door of the lower suite opened and he appeared, his face one big glow of happiness. Behind him, Mollie had that same glow, her gaze hardly leaving him as he said, "I'm ready. Sorry to keep you waiting, Kelvin, but—"

"I heard," Kelvin said as the Percheron shifted his huge feet. "Will we be hearing something about this in church?"

"As soon as I talk with the bishop," Dean said, unable to keep the grin from his face. "I'll come, though I can't promise you'll get much useful work out of me today."

"I'll put you to sweeping floors," Kelvin said. "Not much harm a man can do there."

"I'll finish the sidewalks here," Cora said. "*Denki*, Simon."

"That's very kind of you, Simon," Mollie called. "Maybe we can thank you with supper this week."

"Only if Dean comes, too," Simon teased.

Mollie blushed. "That goes without saying."

Laughing, Simon handed the snow shovel to Cora. "See you soon."

"I guess you will," she said.

Which didn't promise much, but just before the wagon took them out of sight down the road, he looked back. She was still at the end of the sidewalk.

And when he lifted a hand to wave, she waved back.

WHEN CORA FINISHED CLEARING the walks and put both broom and shovel in the shed, Mollie met her in the kitchen as she took off her coat. "Oh, Cora, it's been a long time since I've been so happy. Not since Jeremy was born. I feel as if this one body can't contain it all."

Cora laughed and hugged her close. "You've waited a long time to come out of the valley of the shadow. Just enjoy it. Revel in it. Be like a hen in a dust bath and wallow in it."

Mollie's eyes twinkled. "You have such a way with words." She picked up the teapot that Cora had left abandoned on the counter and forgotten. "Let's make some tea and you can help me make plans." While the kettle boiled, she hunted up some paper and a couple of pencils. "Goodness me. I'm so *verhuddelt* right now I can't remember anything I did for my first wedding."

"If not yours, then how many other weddings have we been to?" Cora teased, getting down the mugs and pouring a dollop of milk and a spoonful of honey into each.

"Lots, but going to one and being in on the planning of one are two different things. How I wish Mamm were here!"

"That should be the first thing on your list—writing to your brothers. And you should tell Aendi Kate and Uncle Jeremiah, too, before it's published in church."

"More than that, we should talk with Aendi Kate." Mollie pointed the pencil at her as Cora poured the tea. "The third of our four cousins was married last winter, so she has lots of experience. She only has Esther at home now."

"Good idea. What about Cousin Esther for *Neuwesitzer?*"

Mollie nodded. "Will you be my *Neuwesitzer,* too? I don't have sisters, but if I did, I wouldn't feel as close to them as I do to you."

Cora couldn't help it. She hugged her cousin again, then set a mug of tea at each of their places before she sat down herself. "Are you sure? Because I—oh, I hate to say this at such a happy time, but honestly, Mollie, I need to start thinking about going home."

"And you can. After my wedding. At which you and Esther will stand up with me."

She had to laugh at a tone that brooked no argument. "All right. Luckily it seems both you and Dean don't plan to wait for spring thaw before you get busy."

"Not a chance. In fact, let's ride over to Aendi Kate's tomorrow and tell them, and then ask if I might be married from there. Just a small wedding." She looked down into her tea. "I mean, neither Dean nor I are spring chickens, and with me being a widow..."

"Let's do that," Cora agreed. "It's a *gut* idea."

"There's one more thing." Mollie hesitated, which was unusual for her. "I have a special request."

"Don't ask me to help pick your colors." Cora waved her hands as though to shoo the thought away. "That's the bride's prerogative."

"*Neh*, nothing like that. I wondered if ... you would write us a wedding song."

Cora gazed at her, feeling as though her insides might collapse. "Oh, Mollie."

"Please? You know me better than anyone, especially after the past few weeks, and you've gotten to know Dean as well. You know what our struggles have been, and our joys."

Talk about struggles and joys. Cora tried to choose among the refusals dancing on the tip of her tongue. But what came out instead was, "I've lost my music." Her throat closed and she put her tea down before she spilled it.

"What do you mean, *Liewi*?" Mollie whispered.

"When Simon—when he—" She took a deep, shuddering breath. "I haven't heard the music, never mind written anything, since the summer."

But Mollie's gaze didn't hold recrimination, or surprise. Instead, her eyes held only sympathy. "Then never mind. We'll find a hymn we both like. I won't put you in that position."

But as they went back to Mollie's list, and Cora recovered enough to smile and even tease her cousin, she couldn't shake the thought—was Simon really responsible for silencing the music in her soul?

Or was the problem really her own unwillingness to forgive *and* forget? Her pride at being treated like she didn't matter?

After all, the Bible said that man was to love a woman the way Christ loved the church, and gave himself for it.

Simon was giving of himself this morning. And in other ways since I've been here. Maybe Mollie is right. He's changed. Or been changed by a Hand greater than any on earth.

And if that was true, what then?

AFTER LUNCH, Cora was still struggling with that question. After the snowfall that had caused all the trouble last night, the sky had cleared and the sun was doing its gentle work on the drifts, making their surfaces gleam. Maybe they'd get a brief thaw.

"I'm going for a walk," she said to Mollie. "I need to think."

"See you when you get back." That was one of the things Cora loved about her cousin. She understood the need to think things through sometimes. "If you pass a phone shanty, give Aendi Kate a call—but don't tell her what it's about. Just that we want to come over for a visit."

"I'll leave all the surprising to you," Cora promised.

The path down on the creek bank, of course, was snowed in, though from up on the bridge, Cora could see the tracks of squirrels and birds criss-crossing the snow. The creek ran through the fields belonging to one of the *Gmee*, and it looked as though someone had taken their sleigh out. Each of its tracks was wide enough for one person to walk in, following the line of trees that bordered the shallow ravine of the creek bed. Cora rambled along it with no destination in mind.

Unless solitude was a destination.

Lord, help me to know what to do. My soul longs for your will … my heart longs for Simon … and my head says 'Don't trust him for a minute.' I'm listening, Father. I want to hear your voice, to feel your hand guiding me in the way I should go.

Her booted foot struck a rock hidden under the packed snow and she danced a couple of steps to regain her balance.

Has it been my hardness of heart all this time, Lord? He has asked forgiveness twice now and I haven't given it. Not completely. It's been lip service. Is that what has made the music go silent and taken your gift from me?

Tears rose in her eyes at the thought, making the light split and refract. She used one end of her black knitted scarf to wipe them away.

Had she brought this on herself?

Mei Vater, hilfe mich, for I know not what I'm doing.

In the creek bed, under the snow, the water chuckled. It looked frozen, buried under a foot of snow at least, but she could hear it. It sounded like a happy baby, gurgling and singing to itself whether anyone was there or not. A sparrow whistled, a stave of notes that told her the tiny creature was glad to see the sun. She squinted into the leafless tree above her head and located its speckled brown body. It sang again, the soprano notes falling into the ravine where the creek kept up a steady alto. Another sparrow across the creek sang back. A rock turned over underwater with a bass sound. On the road, out of her sight, a buggy horse trotted by, *clip-clop clip-clop*, and at the same time, in the top of the tree she was leaning on, two branches rubbed together with a creaking sigh.

The world was alive with music.

She'd just been so wrapped up in herself she hadn't been listening.

Just for fun, she sang the notes the sparrow had sung a moment ago. It sang back, and so did the bird across the creek. Her own delighted giggle added itself to the music. And in the next moment, she was ambushed by song.

> I have always seen you
> Though you were far away
> Walking with me in my mind
> Talking every day.

The stave of the sparrow's notes fell again into the surprised silence of her senses, as though *der Herr* were taking a moment to give her a correction. She changed the melody of the first line to match.

> Each battle that I fought
> I thought I fought alone
> But you were there beside me
> Encouraging me on.
>
> I have always seen you
> Not as you really are
> But as the Father sees you from above;
> You have always seen me
> Through my faults and fears
> Caring for my soul with all your love.
>
> Now we are together
> We've vowed to see life through
> The road that's set before us
> Is wide enough for two.

Cora's throat closed on a sob of gratitude. For here it was, coming unannounced the way the Spirit always did, giving her

Mollie's wedding song ... as well as the song of a soul joyfully recognizing the necessary companion of its walk through life—its loving Elder Brother.

She gazed up at the sky, arching like a vault over her head, and let the sun fall warm upon her face. *"Denki,"* she whispered. "Thank you for giving it back to me."

The giving was done. Now all that was left was the forgiving.

Dear Hannah,

Wow, sounds like you're really putting down roots there. A coffee stand in the Amish Market and a good deal on equipment—congratulations. At least when you get married to some nice Amish guy who won't make you sleep in the back of a car, you'll be able to make him a decent cup of coffee.

Things here are pretty much the same, only different, if that makes any sense. Devon Perch got it together long enough to sign the contract for an exhibition. He left it on the table for so long it got covered up with stuff and finally I fished it out and mailed it for him. He nearly fired me. Said I was messing with his business. I couldn't figure that out—he'd signed the thing, so why not send it? But he said it needed a cooling-off period, whatever that is. Anyway, it's done and now he's mad at me because he has to paint some new canvases.

He says I have to be a subject. Callie too, since she found the stamp to put on the envelope. We're both in the soup, but Callie less than me because he's getting really attached to her cooking. He'd turf me out in a second, but for Callie's eggs Benedict, he says, he'll suffer the slings and arrows of outrageous fortune. Callie says that's from

Shakespeare. I always thought it was the Bible. She read me the speech from the play, and I have to say she's almost as good at reading aloud as she is at cooking.

This must be my week for education. She found out that I'd never seen the Star Wars movies. Devon couldn't believe it either. So we spent the last four days bingeing all nine movies, plus a couple extra ones that fill in the gaps. I can't say I understand all the spaceship stuff and have a hard time keeping all the characters straight, but it's fun. I like the middle ones best. It was easier to figure out what was going on. Devon and Callie know one of them off by heart, seems like. They said the lines right along with the actors. Some people might think that was annoying, but I didn't. Maybe it was the margaritas.

Anyhow, Callie says we're going to watch The Mandelorian next. At least now I know what that is. Probably you do already, but it was all new to me.

Speaking of margaritas, I got paid again, despite sending off Devon's contract without permission. So I finally have enough money to put a radiator and some tires on the Valiant. It's a relief to know that once that's done, I could leave if I wanted. Not that I want to; I like it here. There are good reasons to stay, but it's always nice to leave the back door open.

Give Sallie a hug when you see her. Congrats again on the coffee stall. I hope you do well.

Adios,

Ben

&.

G ood reasons to stay?" Samuel looked up at Hannah, Ben's letter in his hands. "What does that mean?"

It was Saturday, and they sat in the hayloft on a couple of handy bales near the upper window and the hay hook, where the sun pouring in was almost warm. The pile of mail sat beside her, and she'd take it in the house in just a minute, but she'd just had to climb up here to read it. Samuel needed a break from forking hay down through the hay hole anyhow.

"It could mean anything," Hannah said, "but spending all week bingeing movies probably isn't one of those reasons."

"How long is a movie? A couple hours?"

"Some of those are three." She could see her brother doing the arithmetic in his head.

"So ... maybe thirty hours snuggled up on the sofa with Callie is a reason?"

Bang went the nail on the head.

"Maybe she was cooking for part of that time."

"Uh-huh," her brother said. "Which makes another reason."

"You're not making me feel better." She took the letter from him and folded it into its envelope. For the first time, she realized that she'd handed it to him as she would have any message from a friend they both knew. There had been nothing in there that Samuel couldn't read. No sweet little P.S., no paragraph that made her heart go pitter-pat.

Just Callie and her cooking and how she and Ben and Devon Perch seemed to be forming one mismatched, happy family.

"I'm losing him," she admitted, half to herself.

Samuel's hands dangled between his knees. He tilted his head to look at her. "I think he lost you a while ago," he said at last. "When you and me decided to come home and he didn't come along with either of us."

Silently, Hannah acknowledged the truth of this. "Sometimes you're pretty wise, *Bruder*."

"*Neh.*" One of the chickens flew down from the low beam

overhead and pecked in the hay in front of his boots, looking for hayseeds. "Mostly it's knowing Ben pretty well. He just doesn't get that the way he feels now about you is how his family feels every day about him. Knowing that he's not coming back but still hoping that he might."

"How our family felt, hey?" She remembered the lantern Mamm had kept lit in the kitchen window all those years, hoping it would help her and Ashley find their way home. "My sudden departure wasn't really my fault. But did you think about it when you jumped the fence—how Mamm and Dat and the kids would feel?"

"Sometimes," he admitted. "A lot of times. It's hard not to, if you love them."

"Doesn't Ben love his family?"

"You'd know that better than me," her brother said. He moved his feet and the chicken skittered out of range, then resumed hunting. "You guys spent hours talking."

But oddly enough, not about his family, nor how he felt about them. "We talked about what I'd missed growing up. About our family, not his. I mean, his dad drove him crazy and he was glad to be away from that. And I know he loves his *Schweschder* Sallie. But Samuel—" She leaned back on her hands. "How can anyone not love Evie Troyer? Aside from our mom, she's about the sweetest person in the *Gmee* and she adores him. Every time I see her she can't help herself—she always asks me if I've heard from him and if he's okay."

"Luckily you can answer yes to both those questions."

"But I have a feeling the time is coming when I won't be able to. After all, why write to an old girlfriend when you're bonding with the new one?"

Samuel glanced at her again. "Does it bother you? That he might be moving on?"

She had to think past the jumble where her heart was and have a good look around for the truth. "It's funny. I spent all this time this past week thinking about opening the coffee stand on Monday. About designing a quilt with squares pieced like coffee pots to hang up on the wall behind the counter. About how we'll only be open for a month and then the Market closes again until May and how that sucks when I want to do this. In all that time it only occurred to me once to wonder if I'd get a letter that day."

Samuel nodded. "That's kind of an answer, ain't it?" He gave her a smile. "I'm pretty much done here. I'm going to oil tack. If you can lay your hands on a twin, send him out to help me, okay?"

"*Ja.*" She collected the mail off the bale beside her, dusted off the back of her purple dress, and climbed down the ladder to return to the house.

Barbie and Mamm were in the kitchen, assembling a casserole for lunch. Mamm's sharp eye didn't miss the envelope with Ben's handwriting as she took the rest of the envelopes and circulars from Hannah. "News from out west?"

"Not really news," she said. "More of the same, but different."

"But he's all right?"

Hannah nodded. Then she looked up from her contemplation of his spiky, messy handwriting. "Mamm ... how do you know when you've fallen out of love?"

At the counter, Barbie stopped grating cheese and turned to hear the answer.

Mamm gazed at Hannah in some surprise. "I don't really know, *Liewi.* I don't think I ever have."

"Oh, come on. You must have dated before you started going out with Dat."

"Well, sure. But that was the reason I *started* going out with Dat. Because I couldn't see myself in love with any of those other boys. But within a week or two, I knew that if I was going to spend the rest of my life with anyone, it was going to be Jonathan Riehl."

"You knew that within a couple of weeks?"

Mamm smiled a faraway kind of smile, and Hannah could swear a flush of color swept over her cheeks. "I have a little secret. I cared about your Dat before he ever asked me out. So really, I've loved him for longer than I haven't. Which doesn't answer your question at all, does it?"

Hannah had to laugh. "It's a better answer than it deserved, I guess."

"Aren't you in love with Ben anymore?" Barbie sounded hesitant, as though she thought Hannah might get annoyed with her for butting in. "Is that why you asked?"

Hannah could feel the answer before she said it out loud. "I was in love with him, I think. But I'm figuring out that being in love and really loving someone are two different things. They must be, right? Because if I loved him, I wouldn't have left him, right?"

"Weren't you sleeping in the car?" Barbie said skeptically. "And not getting enough to eat? It would take a lot of love to put up with that."

"Maybe I'm shallow," Hannah said, trying to make a joke of it. She didn't feel disloyal to Ben, exactly, letting her sister criticize him. Besides, how could it be criticism if it was the truth? And there were other truths—like Hannah out there by herself, pounding the sidewalks of Venice Beach and La Jolla looking for a job. If he'd cared for her, truly, they would have been looking together. The Amish taught their boys that they were to provide for a family. But Ben could barely provide for himself.

"You are not shallow," Barbie said fiercely, swooping in for a hug. "You deserve a nice man who will make a home for you."

"But what if that's not what I want?" she said, the words coming out of her mouth from nowhere. "Does every Amish girl have to settle down with a nice man?"

"Don't you want to?" Barbie's eyebrows rose.

"I don't know," Hannah admitted. "Mostly I just want to make a life here, with my family and the church. Sell coffee to people. Have good friends like you and Sallie. Not think about marriage and children and all that stuff."

Mamm put an arm around her shoulders. "To answer your question, *neh*, not every Amish girl marries and has children. Those are blessings that *der Herr* wills. And if it's His will for you, then it will happen. The point is to be in the center of that will, so you know right through to your heart that you're doing as He wants, not as you or any of us or the church wants."

Hannah's arms slid around her mother's waist, and she hugged her back. *"Denki,"* she said. "Baby steps, *ja?"*

Maybe she'd take the buggy over to visit Sallie this afternoon, and ask for her help in designing that coffee-pot quilt. And if the bishop was home, she could ask him if her *Deitsch* was good enough now to start baptism classes in the spring.

Baby steps. Away from Ben. And toward the life that God had originally wanted for her.

SIMON CONTEMPLATED the row of silvery pipes lying on the workbench in front of him, the result of several hours at the library computer looking up how to make wind chimes, then carefully measuring twice and cutting once so that each chime yielded the exact tone he wanted. Days of work, sometimes only a few minutes at a time as he'd fit the project around the actual work at the smithy. He didn't want to make Kelvin so impatient that he'd forbid him the use of the tools for the project. He'd messed up the first pipe, but he'd quickly converted it to the smallest, so that as little metal as possible would be wasted, and cut the next more carefully. The other day, Dean had helped him punch holes in the tops for the filament each chime would hang from, and he'd just finished two hours of sanding the ends and the insides of the holes to a silky smoothness.

There would be no rough or sharp edges to hurt the hands hanging it up. But whose hands would they be?

He and Dean had come in to make up the time they'd spent at the bakery yesterday getting Dean safely engaged to Mollie. They'd assembled a gate that was waiting on order, but once that was done, Dean had gone off to see Mollie and Simon had turned to his project. He had the shop to himself, and should be able to finish it today.

His gaze fell on the spool of filament waiting on the bench beside the pipes ... and the ceramic disk Henry had given him that morning.

"I made this for you," his stepfather had said in his quiet way. "They call them wind catchers, or sails, the bit that hangs down through the middle to make the clapper move against the chimes."

Simon turned it over in his hands. It was about the size of his palm, glazed in shades of blue and green. Modeled in relief on both sides were a pair of birds. "Mounting up on wings as ... meadowlarks," Simon murmured. "To sing."

Henry had smiled. "Exactly. The way she does."

"*Denki*, Henry," Simon had said. "This is perfect. But what if I don't give the chimes to Cora? What if I've changed my mind and want to give them to Mollie and Dean as a wedding gift?"

"Then all the more reason to sing," Henry had said. He had squeezed Simon's shoulder and gone off to his shop, whistling the notes of "Walk a Little While."

The chimes would make a *gut* wedding gift for Mollie and Dean. They planned to be married as soon as they could, and until this morning, he'd believed there wasn't time to make another set for Cora.

But he had planned them all along as a gift for her. The chimes sang the first notes of her own song. How could he give them to someone else?

You planned them for a going-away gift. So she wouldn't forget you. But now she's staying to be Neuwesitzer for Mollie, Dean says. You have time.

But he wanted to see her face when she unwrapped it, when she heard the familiar notes playing. To imagine her back at home, hearing the sound on a summer's day, bringing him to mind every single time the wind blew through them and made them sing.

He wanted.

Bring *him* back to mind.

Simon put down the ceramic sail in horror. Had he really just made this gift for her all about himself?

He groaned and plunked down on the stool in front of the bench. Cora was right. Despite his prayers, despite his conviction that he had felt God's hand working with him, molding him, directing him in the way he should go, he *still* carried this fault around inside. Would he ever overcome it?

She had hated it when he'd played her music on the mouth

organ at the pond hockey game. And rightly so. It had been all about *him* showing her he could play her song, not about the song itself, or encouraging the others to learn the words to help them in their walk with God.

And now here he was, about to make the same mistake again. His skin went cold at the thought of what she would say if she ever found out. The merest hint—the smallest suspicion —that he'd made the wind chimes to make her think of him? Why, they'd be shoved back in his hands before you could say *self-centered idiot.*

That decided him.

He would give the chimes to Mollie and Dean. Dean hadn't seen the meadowlark sail, and neither of them would know that Henry had fashioned it with any meaning other than to show a creature that gave its song to God. Mollie might recognize the tune, or she might not. Chimes made random patterns, anyway. She might not even detect that there was a tune, just that the intervals sounded nice no matter which way the wind blew.

The relief that trickled through him told him he'd made the right decision. What was that proverb Daadi Isaac used to say when he was a child? *Experience is a hard teacher. She gives the test first, then the lesson afterward.* Well, there was no doubt in Simon's mind he'd failed the first test, there at the frozen pond. Was it the grace of *Gott* that he'd learned the lesson just in time to pass the second test?

He could only hope so.

He took a deep breath, measured a length of filament according to the list he'd written out, and began to thread the chimes. By the time he had the third one tied in place and hanging from the top ring, they were gently striking each other and he could hear the music.

Simon couldn't think of anything more appropriate than a gift made by the people around them—music for Dean and Mollie's home, composed by Cora, shaped into physical form by his own hands, and turned into art with the addition of Henry's meadowlarks.

Mounting up on wings of song.

❧ 18 ❧

Aendi Kate and Onkel Jeremiah had invited Mollie and Cora to dinner without hesitation, and from the number of buggies in the yard, all their cousins and spouses had come as well. Almost as if they knew there was family news.

"Did somebody tell them?" Mollie whispered to Cora as they put their coats in the bedroom behind the kitchen.

"I didn't," Cora said. "Maybe Kate heard something in my voice. Or the Amish grapevine is more up to date than we thought."

"They won't mind me barging in on a family dinner, will they?" Dean asked.

"Of course not," Mollie told him, taking his black felt hat and hanging it carefully on the peg with his coat in a very wifely fashion. "If you're not family now, you will be by dessert."

They'd met him on the road as they'd turned out of their own drive, and it had taken about two seconds to convince him that his timing was perfect, and he should come along to dinner. Luckily the Jeremiah Swarey household didn't expect their guests to be spit shined and polished, since Dean had said he had been in to the smithy to finish a project and had left Simon there still working. In another ten minutes he'd helped them put their horse back in his stall and had helped them up into his own buggy, and here they were as if they'd planned it all along.

Dean was greeted with what Cora thought was familial cordiality. Someone must have spilled the beans—the Zucker girls? Aendi Kate and her four daughters left the kitchen to join them as Cora, Mollie, and Dean greeted the rest of the family in the living room.

"Mollie, I believe you have some news to share with us?" their aunt said, looking as though she were about to burst with anticipation.

"Why, in fact I do," Mollie said. "There's going to be a new coffee stand opening in the Amish Market on Monday, did you know? Hannah Riehl is going to run it."

Total silence met this announcement, and then their uncle gave a great bark of laughter. "Good for you, Mollie," he said. "Kate, *mei Fraa*, you deserved that."

"You rascals," Kate said, coming to stand next to Onkel Jeremiah and bumping him affectionately with her hip. "The joke is on me, is it?"

"*Neh, Aendi,*" Mollie said with a kiss. "You're absolutely right." She took her place next to Dean, who looked a little overwhelmed. "Dean has asked me to marry him, and I've said yes. You're the first to know."

"Oh, I wouldn't say that," their cousin Esther told her with a laugh. "I heard it at the bakery this afternoon when I went to get yeast rolls."

"And here we thought we were keeping it a secret," Cora

said, laughing. "But I suppose with all the traffic there yesterday we should have expected it to get out. Poor Mollie has barely had time to say yes and the whole *Gmee* probably knows."

Dean took his future wife's hand. "I suppose I ought to have gone over to the bishop's today, since he'll be at the Willow Creek church tomorrow. But Monday will have to do."

"And you'll be published next Sunday?" Onkel Jeremiah asked.

Dean glanced at Mollie, and said, "*Ja*, we have no reason to wait."

Her face glowed as though a flame had been lit inside her. "And it will be small. Just the family and those from the church who can come. Cora has agreed to stand up with me, and Esther, we'd love it if you would, too."

"Oh my! *Ja*, it would be a privilege," Esther said breathlessly. "We must get fabric and get sewing our dresses, then!"

Mollie gave her a hug. "And Onkel, we—we wondered if—"

"Of course you must be married from here," their uncle said firmly.

"Have you set a date?" Aendi Kate asked.

Cora and Esther followed her aunt and uncle and Mollie and Dean into the kitchen to look at the wall calendar. Square after square was marked with wedding dates—Amanda and Joshua, Byron Lapp's niece, Anna Esch and Neil Wengerd coming up ...

"What about here?" Dean's finger landed on the ninth of February. "Is that too soon?"

Onkel Jeremiah laughed again, and his grandchildren peeked into the kitchen to see what was so funny. "Better ask *mei Fraa* if she can whip up a wedding in only three weeks."

"I can if I have to," Aendi Kate said, "but the better question is, will Mollie be able to go up and down stairs with the ministers, and stand to make her vows?"

Mollie glanced at Cora. "I think so."

"I know so," Cora said. "I've never seen anyone so dedicated to her recovery. You've done so well in three weeks that in six, why, you'll be running up those stairs."

"Just no more washing your face in the snow," Dean said with mock sternness. "I don't think I've recovered from *that* even yet."

Which meant that they had to tell the story of the tumble that had precipitated Dean's proposal, which triggered no end of teasing about who had fallen for whom. And then Aendi Kate realized that no one had taken the roast out of the oven, and Cora and her cousins pitched in to rescue it and get dinner on the table. It was a feast in more ways than one. There was a mountain of mashed potatoes with the secret ingredient of cream cheese—which Mollie regretfully had to decline—savory gravy, creamed corn with bits of red pepper for color, green beans with mushroom soup and a crunchy topping of crushed cornflakes, and a colorful jellied salad and bread.

But Cora knew that even if they'd been eating plain cornflakes and skim milk, Mollie and Dean wouldn't have cared. They were sitting together as a couple in the heart of the family—a dream come true for both.

Cora had visited a time or two in recent years when Mollie had been struggling to overcome her despair and hopelessness. In some of those dark hours she had been convinced that, once her husband and child had been taken from her, she had had all the happiness that she was allowed. And later, that a truly happy marriage was out of her reach because she simply couldn't manage the labor of a household. Cora hadn't known then that Dean Yutzy was the secret that had been locked behind Mollie's lips.

Well, now the secret was well and truly out. And despite any moments of doubt her cousin might have suffered, it was clear that the *gut Gott* was showering blessings on her with a generous hand.

After dinner had been cleared away and all the cousins had made short work of the towering pile of dishes, Aendi Kate got out her planning book and invited Mollie and Dean to sit at the table with her. Her daughters couldn't resist the opportunity to chip in hints and stories as Kate consulted her notes and sketched out a plan.

"And don't think you'll escape with just a piece of wedding cake," she called to her sons-in-law in the living room with a mock frown. "We have to get this house cleaned top to bottom, and on such short notice, we women can't do it alone."

"Luckily you fixed the front steps before my wedding," the eldest of their cousins said.

"And painted the house for mine," put in the next eldest.

"We'll need cakes," Kate muttered. "I'll have a word with Carrie Miller, though with all the weddings this winter, she's probably in demand."

"I wondered about cupcake towers instead of cakes," Mollie said softly. "That way, the work can be spread across several households and no one person will need to do it all."

"Ooh, good idea," Kate said, scribbling. "The *Kinner* will love cupcakes."

"Red velvet, for love, with heart sprinkles," the eldest cousin suggested.

"My favorite," Dean said, which decided it.

"Now, we'll need to make the chicken roast the week

before, and creamed celery will do instead of fresh." Aendi Kate muttered as her pencil flicked down the page, making a menu.

"What are your colors?" Esther asked.

"I have no idea," Mollie said. "I just got engaged yesterday."

"We'll let you know," Cora said to them. "At least Mollie's dress is straightforward. We can get blue fabric for the three of us on Monday, and some white organdy for a new cape and apron for Mollie."

"But—" Mollie began.

Already Aendi Kate was shaking her head, as though she had read Mollie's mind. Her niece had, after all, worn wedding clothes before. "All new clothes for an all new marriage, *Liewi*, from the skin out. You know the tradition."

Mollie blushed scarlet at their aunt's plain speaking. *"Ja, Aendi."*

Another hour flew by, and then Esther realized they hadn't even had dessert yet. Kate cut pieces of cherry pie while Esther scooped ice cream on each one and Cora carried them to the living room. When everyone had finished and the plates were cleared away, Onkel Jeremiah stood.

"If we could turn our thoughts to the future while we're all together tonight, and to *Gott*'s hand leading Mollie and Dean, maybe we might pray aloud for them."

Wasn't that just like their uncle, Cora thought—so gruff and down to earth, yet so constant in his belief that God belonged in all the ceremonies of life, both great and small. They knelt on the floor in front of their chairs, the *Kinner* kneeling by their parents, and as each one lifted their hearts and quiet voices in prayer for the newly engaged couple, Cora's heart filled with gratitude. When her turn came, she was ready.

"Dear Lord, thank you for bringing us all together tonight to share our joy with the two you have brought together in accordance with your will. We pray that as they walk together through life, that you would be in the middle, holding both their hands. Giving them your strength when the way seems hard. Showing them your love in daily blessings. And most of all, reminding them each morning that you are there with them, a loving Father who only wants the best for his obedient children. We ask this in Jesus' name. Amen."

Next to her, Esther took a deep breath and began to pray. But Cora was not quite finished. In her heart, she added a P.S.

Keep your hand around me, too, Father. Thank you for showing me your will. Please give me the strength and courage to carry it out, no matter what the result might be. Thank you for giving me back my music so that your words can be part of Mollie and Dean's wedding. And thank you for my family, who show me what it means to love and be constant. Amen.

When the family rose to their feet at last, Mollie was brushing away tears. Perhaps being in the center of her family's prayers had scoured away the last of the darkness and loss in her past, leaving only the good memories and the joy as she looked toward the future. Cora could only hope so.

As though everyone realized at once how late they had stayed, there was a flurry of fetching coats and bundling up children and hugs and arrangements to get together over the next week as preparations began. Then Cora and Mollie climbed into Dean's buggy and they were off toward home.

But as they passed through Whinburg, Dean broke off his conversation with Mollie to say in surprise, "The lights are still on in the smithy, and the generator's running. Don't tell me Simon forgot to turn them off."

"He must still be there, working on something," Mollie said. "Though it's after eleven."

And Cora found words coming out of her mouth that she would never have believed possible. "Can you let me down, Dean? I'm sure he's there. I want to talk to him—he can bring me home afterward."

If Dean had any protests to make about that, they were silenced by Mollie's elbow in his ribs. And in a few moments, Cora waved over her shoulder as the buggy moved off.

She slipped through the door into the smithy. It was surprisingly warm. The hearth still glowed, and beyond it, Simon sat at a bench under a Coleman pole lamp, so focused on what he was doing that he didn't hear her come in.

For a moment, she just watched him. Carefully, he knotted what looked like the last of several pieces of filament thread, then picked up a jumble of pipes. They all hit each other at once, their disorganized chiming loud in the silence of the smithy. Gently, Simon laid his hand on them and, using the hook at the top, hung them from the arm of some large tool.

And she realized what she was looking at. Wind chimes.

One after another, Simon tapped them.

Walk a little while ...

Cora's mittened hand flew to her lips as the breath went out of her.

He lifted his head, and she realized he'd known all along she'd been standing there.

"How ... how did you do it?" she asked. "Make steel pipes play my music?"

"A lot of arithmetic," he said. "The longer the pipe, the deeper the note. I had to figure out what the notes were, first. Henry helped with that. And then figure out how long to make the pipe to produce that note."

"Simon," she breathed. "It's *wunderbaar*. Is it for your mother?"

"*Neh.*" He paused, then seemed to change his mind about what he'd been going to say. "It's a wedding present for Dean and Mollie."

A surge of happiness and admiration went through her, like a wave purling in to shore. "It's perfect."

"Look here." With his forefinger, he turned the ceramic disk at the bottom toward her. "This is called the sail. Henry made it."

She came over to look closely. "Larks. Oh Simon, they will love it. The wedding is February ninth, so you've completed it just in time. It must have taken you ages."

"I've had help." The corners of his mouth quirked up. "Little did Dean know he was helping me cut pipes for his own wedding present."

"Pipes are one thing. Putting it all together like this is something else completely. And ... and the tune?"

He touched the pipes with a fingernail, just enough for each one to breathe its note.

Walk a little while ...

"Henry told me about intervals, and how if the notes are too close or too far away, they make a discord. The tune you wrote has notes that are just right."

"Henry is a wise man." She watched the chimes shiver into

stillness. "Too close or too far away, huh? I guess I'll have to remember that."

"Your songs don't make discord," he said. "I've heard your family singing them. I've sung them."

"There is more than one way to make discord." All of a sudden, she couldn't meet his eyes.

"I hope you don't mean you," he said. "It's me who's been doing that. Between us, at least. Cora, I'm so sorry."

This was the third time he had apologized. She couldn't bear it. Not now, after seeing what he was capable of when he put others first.

"I am, too," she said. "Not for what happened in Colorado. But for keeping my unforgiveness in my heart, like the dragons in the storybooks hoard their treasure."

He was silent a moment. Maybe he was picturing her as a dragon. Well, she couldn't blame him.

"You know what they say," he finally whispered. *"The sweetest song comes from a forgiving heart.* And now?"

"I'm tired of discord," she whispered. "I don't want to feel this way any more. I want to feel the way Mollie does—as though everything has begun fresh and new, and there are no more tears."

"There will always be tears," he pointed out. But his voice was a little husky.

"Yes, but the kind you cry alone are a lot more bitter than the kind you cry on someone's shoulder. I'm really tired of the first kind." Had she ever spoken to a man other than her father with this kind of truth? Cora couldn't remember a single instance.

"If—if you wanted a shoulder to cry on, mine is always here." He patted it with a self-deprecating smile, as though he were offering something he'd found at the scratch and dent.

And suddenly the tears welled up, and she sort of tilted forward, and his arms went around her. "I'm so sorry," she sobbed. "I wouldn't forgive you, and I know I hurt you."

"Not near as much as I hurt you," he said against the top of her *Kapp*. "I was a horrible person. I see that now. I don't know how any of you put up with me. How you could possibly see anything in me that would put that light in your eyes. And then that last day, when I made the light go out—" The words choked in his throat.

"Let's not talk about that day. You've changed since then," was all she could get out before her own breath hitched.

"I hope so." He took a shaky breath. "I prayed that He would mold me. And other things. I don't know if He has answered about those things ... yet."

"What things?" She lifted her head, and for the first time found the courage to search his eyes. What she saw there nearly made her breath stop.

She saw his answer before he said it.

"You," he said simply. "To be worthy of you. To be the man you want me to be."

She shook her head. "Not me. To be the man *God* wants you to be."

"In the end, it comes down to the same thing. I can't be one without the other. Because you're the only woman for me, Cora."

How long she'd waited to hear those words! But if the truth were known, a different man was saying them to a different woman. "I've changed, too. Because of my prayers."

"I know." His smile was intimate. For her alone. "You stand up for yourself now. Not in a way that says *hochmut*, but in a way that says, *I'm worthy of respect. I'm a child of God.*"

"You see that in me?" She had felt it, too, but had been afraid to acknowledge it in case it did smack of pride.

"I do. And it made me want to change. That was the first step God needed before he took me in hand and gave me a shake. Though I don't suppose Dean Yutzy would appreciate knowing he was the person to shake me up."

"You should thank him," Cora said, her own smile glimmering to life.

Simon chuckled. "He has better things than me to think about now." He leaned his forehead on hers, the way they'd done so naturally in the beginning. So close that there could be no pretending anymore, no false fronts, no hurt pride. "If I give them these chimes for a wedding gift, can I make a set for you for an engagement gift?"

Her heart nearly stopped. "What do you mean?"

He kissed her eyelids. Her nose. Her jaw. And finally, her lips. Butterfly kisses, so light they were more a promise than a reality.

"I mean, will you marry me, Cora? Will you let me spend the rest of my life proving how much I love you?"

What she had believed to be a burned ember of a heart had already flickered to life with every word he said. Now it burned high and strong in a glow of joy. "Only if you let me prove the same thing to you."

"I will, for as long as God lets us be together."

"I love you, Simon Yoder."

And when he kissed her, it was more than a promise. It was the beginning of a life together, a new life where the past no longer mattered.

And her soul fell up into the stars with his.

❧ 19 ❧

Three weeks later

Dear Hannah,

Thanks for your letter with all its news. Wow, it took me a day or two to absorb it all. So Simon and Cora got back together? Did not see that coming. I've known him all my life and for the most part thought he was a good guy, until he did that to Cora. She's way too good for him. But hey, if she can forgive him, then I suppose it's nobody else's business.

Enclosed is one of Devon Perch's paintings. It's only 8x10 but I liked the octopus and the jellyfish. Maybe you could have it framed and give it to Simon for a wedding present from me. Not your usual practical household implement kind of gift, but it's worth a lot. Devon gave it to me, but he's not really satisfied with it so says he'll paint me another. Crazy guy. The big ones go for thousands of dollars and he just has them randomly stacked all over the house.

And Mollie Graber and Dean Yutzy, huh? I guess their wedding is any day now. I have to say I hardly know them—Mollie always seemed so old to me, I guess because she had a hard time walking and *was a widow, too. Good to hear the surgery was a success. There aren't a lot of things I like about being Amish, but the pool of money for medical bills is a good thing. Out here they don't have anything like that, unless you have health insurance.*

Which I guess I'm going to have to get. I don't really know how to say this, so I'll just write it down and see how it looks. Callie is expecting. We just found out two days ago, so if I sound a little like I got hit on the head, that's why. Devon didn't have much to say about it, but then, he's up to his ears in oil paint and the real world doesn't actually exist for him at the moment. Callie's pretty happy, and I guess I will be, too, when I get over the shock. Me, a father by fall. See, even when I write it down it doesn't look real.

I have no idea what we're going to do. Keep on keeping on, I guess, like the song says. I don't think a baby will prevent Devon from getting his meals on time, and as long as he pays Callie and me, we can support him or her. Once the show is over and Devon returns to this planet, things may change, but for now I'm happy to just stay here. I'm planning to plant a proper vegetable garden in March or so, where the hippies originally had theirs. That should keep us in carrots and kale for the rest of the year. Callie wants to make her own baby food from organic vegetables. So it will all work out.

I probably won't have time to write much after this, but I wanted to send the painting along for Simon and Cora. If you're ever out this way, we'll be glad to see you, but it doesn't sound like that will happen. I hope you'll be happy being Amish. Like you say, it's what you were meant to be. Just like I was meant to be Englisch.

Have a good life, Hannah. You deserve it.

Ben and Callie +1

The morning of February ninth dawned clear and cold, in a glow of pink over the purple, snow-covered hills. Cora drove Mollie to her wedding in the buggy Onkel Jeremiah had lent them, and behind them came the Zucker sisters in their delivery wagon. Cora devoutly hoped that the wagon wouldn't so much as wobble in a rut. It was loaded with cupcakes of every color and flavor—the Zuckers' wedding gift. All that remained was for the towers to be built on tri-level cake plates in the *Eck*, with more on each table as centerpieces once the wedding service was over.

They arrived at the Swarey place at eight o'clock. One of Kate and Jeremiah's grandsons was acting as hostler for the first time, and carefully led their horse away to be unhitched and stabled, for the snow was still too deep to turn the animals into the pasture outside.

"You look so happy," Cora whispered as they took off their coats in the back bedroom.

"I am," Mollie whispered back. "I'm just glad we got the apron finished in time."

Cora had never had any doubt. Mollie was the kind of person to whom "in time" meant a week in advance. Cora had been to a wedding once where the bride was being stitched into her cape at breakfast on her wedding morning. But luckily, most Amish women around here would have pitched in to help long before that kind of disaster could happen.

Cora wanted to add that Mollie looked beautiful. But she thought she might just leave that for Dean's eyes to say as he gazed at his bride across the aisle. Cora was pretty sure he knew now that Mollie had cared for him for years, even as she gave up hope that he would come back and finally made a different choice. But even if he didn't know that, in spite of it all, their silent gazes would speak volumes.

Half an hour later, after the congregation was seated, the *Neuwesitzern* took their places at the front, facing each other before the ministers. And here Cora was, across the aisle from Simon. It was still hard to believe that Dean had asked him to be his *Neuwesitzer*, along with a cousin from the family connection he'd been staying with. Sometime before spring planting she and Simon would be where Dean and Mollie were now, in the *Abrot,* upstairs with the ministers during the first two hymns receiving instruction about marriage and the way it helped to cement the life of the community.

Next week, once Mollie and Dean began their honeymoon visits, Cora would go back to Colorado to prepare for their own wedding, while Simon worked long hours at the smithy to cover Dean's work and his. Strangely, he was looking forward to it.

"I want to learn as fast as I can so that I can open my own smithy in Amity," he'd told her the other night as they were making plans. "It will cost a bit to start up, so I'll be saving as much of my wages as I can to buy some of Kelvin's old equipment."

"I'll ask Dat to put the word out about a location," she promised. "Or once the King brothers finish Joshua and Amanda's house this summer, maybe we can talk to them about building a shop on Dat's place."

There were so many plans to make. So much joy to look forward to. But as the *Vorsinger* sang the first notes of the wedding hymn, Cora felt her soul swell with the simple joy of raising her voice to the Lord. They knew the hymn by heart— it began every wedding in Lancaster County.

Er hat ein Weib genommen,
Die Christlich Kirch im Geist,
Die Liebe hat ihn drungen,
Die er uns auch hat g'leist.
Sein Leben hat er vor uns g'stellt,
Die ihm auch also lieben
Sind ihm auch auserwahlt.

He has taken a wife
The Christian Church in the Spirit,
The love that so compelled him
He also gave to us.
Before us he's laid his life,
So those who likewise love him
Are also chosen for him.

Together, Cora and Simon gazed into each other's eyes and sang the words that were almost like a vow.

DURING THE LAST verse of the *Loblied*, Samuel Riehl watched Mollie and Dean come in and seat themselves between their *Neuwesitzern*, across the aisle from each other. He had known Mollie Graber all his life, but he had never seen her look the way she did today. Her face simply glowed, and while she was the kind of woman who would never stare all moony-eyed at her husband-to-be while the ministers were sitting right there, everyone in the room could see both the modesty in her bowed head and the joy in her face.

Samuel was happy for her. She'd been through a lot. Not like his sister Hannah, mind you, but he supposed that physical pain and emotional pain could probably inflict equal amounts of damage. But here, today, was a time for healing.

How many weddings had he attended, and never once thought of them in terms of healing? But there at the front was Mollie, proving it. And over on the women's side was his sister, looking every bit as Amish as Sallie Troyer beside her, or Dora Zucker one row behind. Her hair was long enough now that no bits and strands fell out when she put it up under her heart-shaped *Kapp*. And no longer did she peer at the *hoch Deutsch* words in their impenetrable script in the *Ausbund,* trying to figure them out. Instead, she listened to those close by her and sang along, the way she'd done as a small child.

His sister had brought herself back to the fold. Their younger sister Ashley might still be a lost lamb as far as their parents were concerned, despite the fact that she was in college, but they still held out hope that she would choose some day to come back. Hannah, it seemed, had already chosen. She'd had a talk with Bishop Troyer and had told their parents that she was to begin baptism classes in the spring. Mamm had burst into tears over her beef stroganoff, and Dat had too. He hadn't seen his father cry since that awful day they'd had to go to the sheriff's office and report Hannah and Leah-who-became-Ashley missing.

But both terrible grief and grateful joy made his father weep. Maybe there, too, God had finally brought healing.

Hannah had reserved part of her conversation with the bishop for Samuel's ears alone.

"Samuel, if I never have to see a man's face look like that ever again, it will be too soon," she'd told him quietly about a week after her visit, when they'd managed to find a quiet place to talk—this time on the way home in the buggy from the Amish Market, where he'd picked her up. "When was Ben ever going to tell his parents about their first grandbaby? Maybe he'll be mad at me for being a—okay, what's that great word you taught me? A *Plappermaul*. But I don't care. When the bishop asks you point blank what you've heard from his eldest son, what can you say?"

"That he's fine?" Samuel had suggested. "Planning a big garden?"

Hannah had gazed at him sternly over a pair of imaginary glasses. "A lie by omission is still a lie."

Samuel had nodded. "I know. I'd have done the same. I'm glad I didn't have to, though."

"It was hard. And then Evie today, being so sweet about helping with the coffee-pot quilt, and all the while I know she's dying for every detail I can tell her about Caledonia and —and making baby food from organic vegetables."

"Lots of Amish women do, you know."

"Do they?" Hannah thought this over. "Hm. I wonder why no one has opened a shop specializing in organic baby food?"

He laughed. "One thing at a time. Coffee's doing well, *nix*? You still had a line at closing time."

"That's the end-of-a-cold-day commute crowd. They show up exactly twenty minutes' drive from Lancaster on their way home." She'd flashed a sudden smile at him. "I have regulars already. How about that?"

Sitting on the hard bench as the bishop began the first sermon, detailing marriages in the Bible from the beginning, Samuel had to smother a smile at the memory of his sister's delight.

And then Dora Zucker turned her head just enough to catch the tail end of that smile. Their gazes locked for one second.

Just enough to make a tingle run through his entire body.

She blushed and ducked her head, looking as though she were praying or listening to the bishop with all her might and would never *think* of looking at a boy during the marriage sermon.

Dora had a smile that could change a man's whole day. His whole week. His whole life.

Samuel thought he might pay a call on the bishop, too. It would be kind of fitting if he and Dora and Hannah all took classes together, and were baptized on the same Sunday in spring.

And then he would ask Dora if she would like a ride home with him.

ê.

SARAH BYLER, the *Dokterfraa*, felt the flutter deep in her belly as the bridal party took their places in the *Eck* after the wedding. Since the crowd was comparatively small, both wedding and the meals would take place in the house. She grabbed Henry's hand and dragged him into the bathroom with her.

"Are you all right?" he whispered.

"*Ja*, we both are. Feel." She covered his hand with her own, flattening it over the slight roundness of her belly.

An expression of wonder crossed his face as he felt it, too. "Our baby must like weddings."

"A girl, then, for sure and certain," she said with a grin.

He took her into his arms and kissed her. "I wouldn't be so certain about that. I think our Simon can't wait for his own."

He led her out of the bathroom before someone pounded on the door, and they found their place at one of the tables reserved for the parents of all the wedding party.

There was her Simon beside the groom, using a cupcake tower as cover to lean over to whisper something to Cora. As though he couldn't get enough of sharing this joyful day with her.

"I have never seen my boy so happy," she whispered to Henry as people seated themselves all around them, pushing back benches with a squeak, managing children, chattering with friends.

"And seeing him happy makes you happy, which makes me happy," Henry replied, capturing her hand again under the tablecloth, as though they were a courting couple paired off at the wedding supper.

She searched his face, those dear eyes, the beard that he despaired of because it wouldn't grow in evenly. "And you?" she asked. "Are you happy with the choices you've made?"

"You know I am." His very gaze was a kiss. "I came here as shabby and lonely as poor Aendi Sadie's farm. And now look at me. I have a beautiful wife, two boys who love God, and a *Boppli* on the way who will definitely be a girl. You'll be teaching her the wonders of herbs and gardens by the time she's three, I know it. God has been good to us, Sarah."

"Bless Aendi Sadie," Sarah said, squeezing his hand. "She knew what she was doing when she left you the farm and dragged you out here from Denver."

"She was a canny one," he agreed. "And God used her love to multiply it a hundredfold."

"It's what He does." She and Henry. Simon and Cora. Soon, Caleb would be catching some girl's eye and bending Henry's ear about her as they worked together in the pottery. Again, she felt that flutter under her heart.

Love. It was like the seeds she scattered in the spring to create her quilt garden. The more you offered it with an open hand and nurtured it, the more bountiful the harvest the *gut Gott* gave you.

And what a wonderful certainty that was.

§❧

THE BRIDE and groom were going from table to table, greeting their guests and offering them small mementoes of their day—in this case, little bags of candied almonds in the bride's colors, butter yellow and robin's-egg blue.

Amelia Fischer stood with her two best friends, Emma Weaver and Carrie Miller, all of whom went to church with the bride. Carrie had just given them her news.

"Expecting!" Amelia flung her arms around her in a hug. "Oh, how *wunderbaar*! After all those barren years—"

"—you will have three!" Emma hugged her gently in her turn, her own little *Boppli* sleeping on her shoulder.

Carrie's gaze found her husband Melvin in the crowd, their redheaded girl's hand in his while he talked with the deacon, their boy likewise asleep on his shoulder, his long legs dangling.

"It seems a miracle," she said softly. "Not so many years ago all I could think of was what I didn't have. It was a *gut* thing *der Herr* wasn't listening to all my moaning and groaning. He was busy planning so many gifts my heart can hardly hold them all—adopting Rachel, then finding out right after that I was expecting Zeph, and now a third on the way."

"We've been making nothing but baby quilts lately," Amelia teased. "What kind of quilt should we make next? We can't stop now, you know. We started a tradition with Emma's wedding quilt, *Sunrise Over Green Fields*."

"Which I have on my bed and always will," Emma said firmly. "When I think of what we were all going through during the making of it—your diagnosis scare, Amelia, and my belief that I would be single forever because Grant was married, and you, Carrie, a woman made to be a mother who couldn't conceive ..." She shook her head. "All I can say is, we were lucky to have each other."

"It wasn't luck," Amelia said softly. "It was love."

Emma's lips trembled. "You're absolutely right. And it always will be."

Carrie slipped an arm around each of their waists and gave her best friends—her sisters of the spirit, as Melvin's mother said—a squeeze.

And together, they took it all in. The love of the newly-weds as he carried the basket of favors for his bride. The love of the former fence jumper and the *Dokterfraa* as they watched her son whisper in the ear of the woman he would soon marry. The girl who had been taken, and the boy God had brought back, thriving in the love of their family. And the bishop's wife, whose faith in the love of Him who held the *Gmee* and her eldest son in the palm of his mighty hand never wavered.

Somewhere, Amelia thought, she could hear the sound of singing. The *Youngie*, probably, unable to wait for later. God's people, raising their voices in His praise, in the sweetest song of all.

THE END

AFTERWORD

A NOTE FROM ADINA

I hope you enjoyed reading *The Sweetest Song*, the final book in the Whinburg Township Amish series, and catching up with friends from my fictional township in the very real Lancaster County, Pennsylvania. You might leave a review on your favorite retailer's site and tell others about my books. And you can find print and digital editions of my series online. I invite you to visit my website at www.adinasenft.com, where you can subscribe to my newsletter and be the first to know of new releases and special promotions.

Looking for more of my Amish fiction? You'll find Anna Esch and Neil Wengerd's story, "The Heart's Return," in the *Amish Christmas Miracles* collection. And I'm excited to let you know my Amish Cowboys series kicks off with the Miller family of the Circle M Ranch, Montana, in *The Amish Cowboy*. I hope you'll pick it up soon!

Denki!

Adina

GLOSSARY
THE SWEETEST SONG

Spelling and definitions from Eugene S. Stine, *Pennsylvania German Dictionary* (Birdboro, PA: Pennsylvania German Society, 1996).

Abrot pre-wedding consultation with elders
Aendi aunt, auntie
Ausbund the Amish hymnbook
Bischt du okay? Are you okay?
Boppli baby
Bruder brother
Dat Dad
Daadi Grandpa
Daadi Haus grandfather's house
Demut humility
Denki, denkes thank you, thanks
Deitsch Pennsylvania Dutch
Dochder, Dechter daughter, daughters
Dokterfraa female herbalist or healer
Duchly headscarf

Eck corner

Eck Leit lit. corner people, servers at the bridal table

Englisch Someone who is not Amish, the English language

Gehorsamkeit obedience

Gelassenheit letting go of the world

Gesangbuch songbook

Gott God

Gottes Wille God's will

Gmee congregation

Guder mariye good morning

Guder owed good afternoon

Guder nacht good night

Gut good

Haus house

Herr, der the Lord

Himmel heaven

Hinkelhaus henhouse

hoch Deutsch high German

Hochmut lit. highness; being proud

Im e Familye weg in the family way, pregnant

ja yes

Ischt gut. It's good.

Ischt so? Is it so?

Kapp The prayer covering worn by Amish women, which can vary in design from district to district

Kinner children

Kumm mit. Come with me.

Lieber Gott, hilfen mir. Dear Lord, help me.

Liederbuch songbook

Liewi dear, dearest

Loblied hymn always sung second in Amish services

Mamm Mom

Mammi Grandma

Maedel young girl

Maud maid

mei Fraa my wife, woman

mei lieber freind my dear friend

Mei Vater, hilfe mich my Father, help me

Mopskopp stupid fellow

Neh no

Neuwesitzer, Neuwesitzern lit. side sitter(s), supporters of the bride and groom

nix (der. nichts) isn't it

Onkel uncle

Ordnung community rules for living the Amish life

Plappermaul blabbermouth

Schweschder(e) sister, sisters

Onkel uncle

Ordnung Rules of the church community

Rumspringe Lit. running around, the time of freedom for Amish young folks between age 16 and marriage

Uffgeva giving up (of the will)

verhuddelt confused, mixed up

Verschteh? Understand?

Vorsinger fore singer, one who starts the hymns

Was ischt? What is it?

Was tut dich? What are you doing?

Wie geht's? How is it going?

wunderbaar wonderful

Youngie unmarried young people

Zwickel fool

The Smoke River series

Grounds to Believe

Pocketful of Pearls

The Sound of Your Voice

Over Her Head

The Glory Prep series (faith-based young adult)

Glory Prep

The Fruit of My Lipstick

Be Strong and Curvaceous

Who Made You a Princess?

Tidings of Great Boys

The Chic Shall Inherit the Earth

Writing as Charlotte Henry

The Rogues of St. Just series (Regency romance)

The Rogue to Ruin

The Rogue Not Taken

One for the Rogue

ABOUT THE AUTHOR

USA Today bestselling author Adina Senft grew up in a plain house church, where she was often asked by outsiders if she was Amish (the answer was no). She holds a PhD in Creative Writing from Lancaster University in the UK. Adina was the winner of RWA's RITA Award for Best Inspirational Novel in 2005, a finalist for that award in 2006, and was a Christy Award finalist in 2009. She appeared in the 2016 documentary film *Love Between the Covers*, is a popular speaker and convention panelist, and has been a guest on many podcasts, including Worldshapers and Realm of Books.

She writes steampunk and cozy mysteries as Shelley Adina; and as Charlotte Henry, writes classic Regency romance. When she's not writing, Adina is usually quilting, sewing historical costumes, or enjoying the garden with her flock of rescued chickens.

Adina loves to talk with readers about books, quilting, and chickens!
www.adinasenft.com
adinasenft@comcast.net